What happened to Drew?

Her partner could be hurt. Or worse, dead. Bile burned her throat. The thought of losing another partner caved in her heart. But her priority had to be eliminating the danger.

Still in a crouch and leading with a two-handed grip on her gun, she moved slowly in the direction of what she hoped was the front door. She mentally ticked off the steps. The dark overwhelmed her, playing havoc with her equilibrium. She bumped into something solid and froze. Her pulse jumped. Not a wall. There was no furniture.

Panic jolted through her. She jumped away and whipped around, looking for a target. But the blackness concealed the threat.

If it were Drew, he'd say something, right?

The scuff of a shoe on the wooden floor sounded as loud as a gunshot.

"Drew?" she whispered. *Please, dear Lord, let Drew be okay.*

If something happened to him...

Something touched her hair.

Terri Reed's romance and romantic suspense novels have appeared on *Publishers Weekly* top twenty-five and Nielsen BookScan's top one hundred lists and have been featured in *USA TODAY*, *Christian Fiction Magazine* and *RT Book Reviews*. Her books have finaled in the Romance Writers of America RITA® Award contest, the National Reader's Choice Award contest and three times in the American Christian Fiction Writers' The Carol Award contest. Contact Terri at terrireed.com or PO Box 19555 Portland, OR 97224.

Books by Terri Reed

Love Inspired Suspense

Northern Border Patrol

Danger at the Border
Joint Investigation

Capitol K-9 Unit

Duty Bound Guardian

Protection Specialists

The Innocent Witness
The Secret Heiress
The Doctor's Defender
The Cowboy Target

The McClains

Double Deception
Double Jeopardy
Double Cross
Double Threat Christmas

Visit the Author Profile page at Harlequin.com for more titles.

JOINT INVESTIGATION

TERRI REED

HARLEQUIN® LOVE INSPIRED® SUSPENSE

Recycling programs
for this product may
not exist in your area.

LOVE INSPIRED BOOKS

ISBN-13: 978-0-373-44679-7

Joint Investigation

www.Harlequin.com

Printed in U.S.A.

For God has not given us a spirit of fear,
but of power and of love and of a sound mind.
–2 Timothy 1:7

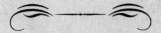

To my husband, who loves and accepts me, flaws and all.

ONE

The smell hit her ten feet from the motel door. Fresh blood. Pungent and tangy. Sticky sweet. A scent once experienced not easily forgotten. FBI agent Sami Bennett's stomach heaved. Anguish fisted in the middle of her chest. Images of arterial spray, unseeing eyes, birds, lots and lots of birds, flashed through her mind like an animated flip book.

Shaking her head to clear the pictures from her brain, she focused on the moment, her hands tightening around the grip of her Glock 23.

Clamping her lips together, she calmed her racing heart and pressed closer to the wall along the shadowy second-story balcony of the cheap motel on the outskirts of Vancouver, British Columbia, Canada. All the bulbs in the wall sconces were broken.

Glass crunched beneath the heels of her black Dr. Martens boots. The cool dark night was ripe with moisture, and overhead thunder rumbled like an angry fist against a wooden drum.

Sami was angry, too. Angry she'd been chasing a phantom for six months who remained one step ahead of her yet had the gall to leave her a trail to follow. Frustration beat at her temple.

She thought of the photocopied postcard in her pocket. The latest clue left by the killer she'd dubbed Birdman because of the image of a small bird, either hand drawn, ink stamped or stickered, found on each clue.

She debated retreat. Most likely Birdman was long gone, leaving behind another dead body and another bread crumb to track. She was so tired of the gore, of the deaths. So tired of being the one to find the bodies.

But if there was the slimmest chance that she could catch Birdman, then she had to proceed. Giving up wasn't an option. She wouldn't rest until the man was behind bars.

She inched closer to the room at the end of the balcony. The air around her shifted as if a hot-breathed creature mirrored her steps. Tensing, she glanced over her shoulder. The world was shrouded in inky darkness. A shiver of apprehension tripped down her spine.

"Lord, please have my back," she whispered.

With laser-like focus, she returned her attention to the door of room 218. Was Birdman in the room? Would she finally catch him?

She hoped so. She wanted this over. She wanted to take the man down. She wanted her life back, but she'd promised to bring her childhood friend's murderer to justice. And she always kept her promises.

Steeling herself against what she'd find inside the room, she reached for the door handle. Through the thin leather gloves she wore, the handle was cool. She turned the knob.

The sound of glass being crushed behind her sent

alarm sliding across her flesh. Before she could react, an arm snaked around her torso, pinning her arms to her sides and rendering her gun useless. A large hand clamped over her mouth, stifling her yelp of surprise.

Panic flooded her system. The world narrowed to one thought—escape.

She kicked and thrashed but the body at her back held her in an unbreakable grip. Her assailant unceremoniously hauled her off her feet and carried her away.

Royal Canadian Mounted Police inspector Drew Kelley gritted his teeth against the onslaught of feisty female in his arms. She packed a mighty hard kick and a mean elbow. Neither of which fazed him enough to loosen his hold. But he'd have bruises for her effort.

Seconds before he'd seen the person wearing an FBI-issued windbreaker sneak up the stairs, he'd heard his American counterpart exclaim through the communication link wedged in his ear, "What's the FBI doing here?"

A good question indeed. The US Federal Bureau of Investigation was not part of this IBETs—Integrated Border Enforcement Teams—task force.

Discovering the intruder was a woman had been a surprise. With his hand still over her mouth to keep her from alerting the drug dealers they were hoping to catch, he carried her down the motel stairs and across the parking lot to another bank of rooms.

His team had commandeered a ground-floor room as their staging area. From there two members of the six-man team watched the parking lot, ready to signal when the fun started and they could move in to take down a drug dealer who was bringing illegal narcotics across the border into Canada.

The Americans had received an anonymous tip that a major drug deal was going down tonight in room 218. However, this woman—this supposed FBI agent—might have messed it all up.

The door to the ground-floor motel room swung open. US Border Patrol agent Luke Wellborn stepped back so Drew and the woman could enter the room. Luke closed the door behind him.

"Get the gun before she shoots someone," he growled to the men inside.

US Immigration and Customs Enforcement agent Blake Fallon quickly disarmed the woman. He set the piece on the dresser and leaned against the wall with his arms across his chest. His hard features settled into cynical annoyance.

Once the door was closed, Drew withdrew his hand from the woman's mouth.

"Put me down!" She twisted her head to glare at him. Her blue eyes sparked, making him think of gemstones in a jeweler's display case, and her lush mouth bunched up with outrage.

Not about to let a pretty face distract him, Drew tucked in his chin to squint down at his charge. "Not yet. Who are you?"

"Special Agent Sami Bennett," she ground out, and wiggled some more, trying to free herself. "My ID's in my back pocket. I'm FBI."

Luke snickered. "Right."

Drew's lips twitched but he held his smile at bay. He understood his colleague's skepticism. Sami Bennett didn't fit his image of a field agent. She was tall for a woman, reaching to Drew's chin, which he estimated made her five-nine, and though there was no ignoring her feminine shape, she was slender, bordering on too skinny.

In addition to the black windbreaker with the FBI logo, she was dressed from head to toe in black.

He reached into the back pocket of her dark cargo pants to retrieve a leather wallet. He handed it off to the other man in the room, RCMP sergeant Justin Lorie.

Behind a pair of thick dark-rimmed glasses, Justin inspected the identification inside. "Appears she's telling the truth." He held up the FBI badge.

Blake snagged it. "We'll see about that." He pocketed the wallet with the badge.

Sami thrashed in Drew's arms. "Hey, give that back."

For all they knew, the ID could be fake. Just because she wore a marked jacket that anyone could order off the internet didn't mean he believed her. Drew gestured toward the table and chairs across the drab, sorely outdated room. "Bring a chair over here."

Justin dragged the closest chair away from the window and set it in front of Drew. Thankfully, it had arms and though the plaid seat cushion had seen better days, the chair would suffice.

Meeting Justin's brown-eyed gaze, Drew conveyed his intent with one word: *"Ties."*

Justin nodded.

Drew set the woman down in the chair and held her arms in place along the armrests.

"What are you doing?" Sami struggled to break free of his hold on her. "You can't do this!"

Justin wound a plastic zip tie over the armrest and one wrist.

"Not too tight," Drew warned, not wanting to damage her skin.

"Hey! Hey, you can't—" she protested.

Justin threaded the end of the tie through the joint, the *click, click* of the tooth sliding along the ridges sounding like nails on a chalkboard. He secured one wrist, then the other.

Pulling against the restraints, the woman shouted, "I'm an American citizen. A federal agent. I'll have your badge for this!" Her bright blue eyes flashed with anger in her attractive heart-shaped face. Blond hair escaped from beneath the black stocking cap covering her head.

"You're not in the United States at the moment. This is my jurisdiction, ma'am," Drew pointed out.

She leveled him with a mutinous scowl. "And you are?"

"RCMP inspector Drew Kelley."

Sami looked at the Border Patrol logo on Luke's jacket, then shot him a dark look. "You're American. Tell him to let me go!"

Luke shrugged, his boyish features conveying empathy. The ten-year USBP veteran looked as if he were fresh out of the academy. A look that fooled many into underestimating him. "Not my show."

"What are Border Patrol and ICE doing here?" She nodded at Blake, who, like Luke, wore a black jacket with his agency acronym emblazoned on the front and back. "A joint task force?"

"The bigger question," Drew said, "is what are *you* doing here?"

She jerked her gaze back to him. "I'm tracking a serial killer. He is, or was, in that room. He's going to get away."

"Serial killer?" He rubbed his chin. If a serial killer were on the loose in his country, his office would know. What kind of ploy was this? His gaze lifted to the other members of the task force. "Do you know anything about this?"

Luke and Justin shook their heads.

"Nope," Blake said, his dark eyes flashing with disdain. "My intel says there's a major drug deal happening tonight at this motel in room 218. She's probably part of it. Maybe a decoy to distract us."

"Your intel is wrong," Sami said. "I'm nobody's decoy. There's a dead body in that room."

"You killed somebody?" Drew asked. For some reason the thought of her as a killer didn't seem right. He shook off the thought. In his experience murderers came in all shapes and sizes. He'd been at this job long enough to not take anyone at face value.

"No," she shot back in a tone that implied he was dense. "Of course not. You stopped me from entering the room, so how could I kill anyone inside?"

Blake shrugged and matched her tone. "Maybe you're coming back to clean up."

"How long have we been sitting on that room?" Drew asked his team.

Justin answered, "Three hours."

Drew stepped toward the window. The view to room 218 was unobstructed. "No one has come or gone?"

"Nope," Blake drawled, his American Southern roots echoing through the word. He pointed a finger at the woman. "Only her."

Sami pulled against the restraints holding her to the chair. "The killer could still be in there."

The agitation in her voice vibrated through the room and settled in Drew's chest.

"You have to listen to me. You need to breach the door and capture him before he slips away." She whipped her gaze to Drew. He sucked in a breath at the pleading look in her eyes. "The victim could be Canadian." Her gaze slid back to Blake and narrowed her eyes. "Or American."

For some reason Drew found himself drawn in by her impassioned plea. He considered his options. They could sit tight and keep watching the room. But his instincts told him this sting was a bust. Either Blake's intel was bad or they'd been made.

Or they could move in now. If they did, then they were ensuring this operation was over, time and resources wasted. Although if what the woman—the FBI special agent—said was true...

He'd been appointed as the lead on the joint binational operation; the choice was his. "We breach the room."

Blake pushed away from the wall, his lip curling. "I'm calling this in."

"After," Drew countered, asserting his authority as he met the ICE agent's intense gaze. This was Drew's op, his country. They'd proceed as he dictated.

Blake's nostrils flared but he conceded with a nod. "Fine. You're the boss...eh?"

His tone made it clear he thought Drew was making the wrong move.

Drew grinned. "That's the rumor."

Blake Fallon scooped up the Glock from the dresser and headed out the door.

If he was making a mistake, he'd deal with the consequences later. For now, Drew was going with his gut. "Let's go."

"What about me?" Sami cried.

At the door Drew paused. "You'll be safe until we return."

"Wait!" Sami gaped at the men's retreating backs. "You can't leave me here!"

The door shut behind them. Unbelievable. Sami stamped her foot with irritation and let out a growl of frustration. How dare the big Canadian treat her like a criminal!

She blew out a breath and calmed herself. Well, she'd show him.

Thankfully, his sidekick had placed the ties far enough up her wrist that she had movement of her hands. She lifted her right foot and set it across her left knee so she could reach her Ka-Bar knife tucked inside a sheath within her boot.

She drew the knife out and maneuvered the blade in her palm so that the flat side lay against her skin. Then carefully she pushed the knife with her fingers down the inside of her forearm beneath the tie.

She rotated the head of the knife until the dull edge of the blade dug into her skin while the sharp side pressed against the tie. Bending her palm, she applied pressure and the knife's sharp edge cut through the plastic tie like butter.

Exhilarated with her success, she quickly sliced through the tie on her right wrist and then ran from the room.

A drizzling rain moistened the air. Not a good night to be outside. Her clothes soaked up the moisture, making her skin prickle and a chill slide across her flesh. She raced across the parking lot, her gaze on the dark balcony, her hand clenching her knife tightly.

Shadows moved along the walkway. The Canadian and his cohorts—ICE and US Border Patrol. Their presence didn't make sense. Was it a coincidence that a joint task force team was staking out the exact place Birdman had led her to? Was Birdman toying with other agencies, as well?

Hurrying up the staircase, she stumbled on the steps. It was hard to see in the darkness, but she didn't dare use the flashlight tucked in one of her pants pockets. As she reached the end of the balcony, the sound of wood splintering echoed through the quiet night. They'd breached the door.

"Halt!" A cry broke through the hushed silence.

A loud thud followed by a yelp of pain revved Sami's blood. Anticipation grabbed her by the throat. Would they catch the killer? Would her nightmare finally come to an end?

"Suspect escaping through the bathroom window!"

She recognized the voice as the younger Canadian Mountie.

The ICE agent doubled back, nearly knocking Sami over as he ran down the stairs in hot pursuit of their quarry.

A light winked on in the room. The bright garish glow should have been welcoming. It wasn't.

She hurried forward; the scent of death assaulted her senses. She gagged but forced herself to step inside the motel room. Would she ever grow accustomed to the smell? She prayed not.

She nudged aside the men. Their bleak expressions

made dread twist in her gut. She followed their gazes to the bed. Though she knew what to expect because she'd seen other corpses, including that of her childhood best friend, the sight of the mutilated woman lying atop the multicolored bedspread made her breath catch and tears burn the backs of her eyes. Her heart sank. Would she ever be able to stop this madman?

Justin stumbled out of the bathroom doorway, holding his bleeding nose. "A guy was hiding in the bathtub. He dived out the open bathroom window."

"And dropped two stories?" the man in charge, Inspector Drew Kelley, questioned. He stood well over six feet, with massive shoulders that filled out the midnight blue uniform beneath his flak vest. He wore his dark hair shorn in a classic clean cut. His hazel eyes reminded her of the leaves in fall.

Justin shrugged, clearly as perplexed as Drew.

"Agent Fallon is in pursuit," Justin supplied.

Drew spoke into a radio attached to his shoulder, his commands sending others on the hunt, as well.

Fury erupted in Sami's chest. If the Canadian hadn't stopped her... She still had a chance to catch Birdman. Sami ran toward the busted hotel room door. Her gaze hit the wall over the bed. Her feet skidded to an abrupt halt.

Defacing the plain white wall was a rudimentary depiction of a set of eyes drawn in bright red. In blood.

The world tilted. Shivers of fear slid along her limbs. She almost dropped her knife. This was an ambush. The killer had anticipated her arrival. He'd wanted her to see that he was in control.

"Out with you," Drew said to Justin. "We don't

need your blood contaminating the scene." Justin left the room.

Drew turned his attention to Luke. "Secure the perimeter. This is a crime scene."

The fresh-faced agent nodded grimly and left to do the big guy's bidding.

Sami met Drew's gaze. He watched her with an intensity that would have unnerved her but she was too freaked out to be fazed.

"How did you…?"

Interpreting his question of how she escaped the ties binding her to the chair, she held up her knife. "Your man didn't do a thorough search."

Irritation flashed in his eyes.

"Why did you think a drug deal was going down here?" she asked.

Drew ran a hand over his stubbled jaw. "US Immigration and Customs Enforcement received an anonymous tip about drugs being smuggled from the US to Canada and a major buy was supposedly taking place here tonight."

"It was Birdman."

"Who?"

"The killer I'm tracking. He killed this woman. And he wanted you here. He wanted me here." Cold fingers of dread traipsed up her back. "He knows I'm after him."

"Why would he call in a phony crime and bring authorities here?" Drew asked.

She stared back at the wall. "I believe you saved my life, Inspector."

"You think he wanted to kill you?"

"Maybe he wants me dead." She lifted a shoulder

to convey she was guessing. "Maybe he wants me to suffer."

"Why?"

"I think because I'm the only one to connect the dots." She turned to stare at the Canadian. The swirling depths of his eyes made her feel dizzy. Her gaze dropped to his mouth, which was set in a hard line.

She forced herself to straighten and meet his stare once again. "He either would have killed me or he would have framed me for this woman's murder." She'd almost walked into his trap. A shiver skated across her nape. "Instead of a drug bust, you'd be arresting a supposed murderer. Me."

"Why do you call him Birdman?"

She tucked her knife back into her boot and then withdrew from her pocket the photocopy of the postcard from the last crime scene. She handed it to him.

Drew studied the image of the same low-budget motel they now stood in.

"Look on the back of the postcard," she instructed.

"'Room 218.'" Grim anger darkened the complexities of his eyes. "That's how you knew to come here."

"Yes. And see the little drawing in the bottom corner?"

"A bird. Crude but identifiable."

"Birdman. All his bread crumbs hold similar images. Sometimes they're hand drawn, as that one is. Sometimes he uses a stamp or stickers with the same type of bird image." An image she couldn't get out of her head. "I've scoured the makers of both the stickers and the stamps, but they're too generic and sold too widespread to be of use tracking down Birdman through his purchases."

Drew's brow creased. "Where did he leave this?"

She inhaled as the crime scene flashed through her mind. "Washington, DC. The postcard was tucked into the shirt of his fourth victim." Her eyes flicked to the bed and back. "This is number eight. As far as I know."

"So he tells you where he'll strike next."

She let out a mirthless laugh. "Or where he's been." A knot twisted in her chest. "The clue on the third victim actually pointed to victim number five. And the bread crumb found at number two led to number six." At Drew's confused looked, she explained. "Time of death confirms the order."

"Why is a lone FBI agent hunting this Birdman?"

A sour taste filled her mouth. When her boss found out where she was and what she was doing…she'd probably find herself in the unemployment line. But that was a risk she was willing to take. "I'm the only one who figured out the deaths are related. All the deaths occurred in different cities, different jurisdictions. I only stumbled across the connection six months ago."

Because of Lisa. Her heart cramped.

Her eyes swept over the room looking for the clue to the killer's next—or already dead—victim.

There, propped up against the television set. A small square object. She sucked in air as dread flooded her veins. From the leg pocket of her pants she grabbed a pair of disposable gloves and slipped them on.

Drew's gaze, homed on her back like a laser, followed her as she walked to the console and gingerly picked up the credit card. She read the name embossed in silver lettering. James Clark.

Her throat closed up. The implications ricocheted

through her mind, setting off clanging bells. A man's credit card?

She flipped the card over. Her heart stalled. A bright yellow sticker of a bird flashed at her like a neon light.

The blood drained from her head, making her light-headed. Slowly, she turned to Drew.

Concern filled his face. "What's wrong?"

"Eight bodies. All women, all killed exactly the same way." She held out the card. "Birdman is changing his MO."

TWO

After donning a glove to keep his prints off the evidence, Drew studied the credit card for a moment before lifting his gaze to Sami. She stood stiff as a board with her fists at her side. Though she tried to hide it, he could see she was wigged out by this turn of events. Her face had gone pasty white. She sucked in air, in and out, in and out.

Unexpected empathy twisted in his gut. The last thing he needed was for her to pass out in the middle of a crime scene and contaminate the evidence. Taking her by the elbow, he propelled her out of the motel room, away from the grisly scene and the eerie drawing on the wall.

"We'll turn the card over to our forensic team when they arrive to process the room and handle the victim," he said once they were on the balcony.

He tucked the credit card inside an evidence bag. According to Sami, the killer's MO was evolving. Birdman, as she'd called him, was becoming more comfortable, more confident. Ready to add men to his repertoire.

It wasn't unusual for a serial murderer to make subtle

changes to their form of homicide as they grew more adept at killing, but a sudden change in gender? That was uncommon, though not unheard of. Was there more than one killer? Were the deaths Sami was investigating even related to the one here?

He couldn't discount the bird image. She believed the bird was the killer's signature. But Drew didn't know what the symbol represented to the murderer.

"We need to run the name on the card." Her terse tone matched the rapid clip of her stride. "Find him. Though it's probably too late."

"The credit card could belong to the victim in this room. Her husband's?" Drew offered, though he doubted his own speculation.

She didn't say anything. She didn't have to. Her certainty wouldn't be swayed. Not that he blamed her. She was obviously committed and passionate about finding this murderer. He appreciated that. Police work took dedication and perseverance. Sometimes to the detriment of everything else in one's life.

He should know. He didn't have much beyond his work. Which was fine with him. He didn't need anything or anyone else. It was simpler not to have a personal life, because outside the job, it was too easy to let his guard down as he had with his ex-wife. He had no intention of letting anyone else rip his heart to shreds.

Once they were in the parking lot, Drew headed for the American agents, Border Patrol Agent Wellborn and ICE Agent Fallon. They gathered with the rest of the IBETs team at the back of a van that housed their equipment. Only a few other cars dotted the parking lot. The motel didn't do a huge business, it seemed, just enough to stay solvent.

Justin's nose no longer bled and thankfully didn't look broken. Drew led Sami to the group of men.

"Did you catch him?" Sami asked Luke, clearly finding him more approachable than Agent Fallon. Drew didn't blame her. Fallon could be intimidating, but Drew also knew he was a good man to have watch your back. Fallon knew how to get a job done.

"No. He escaped," Luke replied, frustration evident in his voice.

"He jumped into a sedan and took off," Canadian Border Services agent Nathaniel Longhorn offered. A First Nation descendant, Nathaniel kept his black hair long and tied back with a leather strap. He was lean, muscular and deadly with a knife. Drew was glad to have him on his team. "I've radioed in the license plate to the Vancouver police and to the border crossing."

"Secure the scene and wait for Forensics to show," Drew instructed. Then he handed the evidence bag containing the credit card to Justin. "Run the name. Find out where this was last used and see if you can track down the man."

Justin peered at the credit card. "Will do."

"Whoever that card belongs to is a potential victim, if not dead already," Sami interjected.

Blake slid his gaze to her. "You sound sure, Special Agent Bennett. And yes, I did check on your credentials." He smirked. "Your boss is eager to talk to you."

Sami glanced at Drew, then back to Blake. "I am sure."

Interesting that she didn't elaborate or acknowledge Blake's remark that her boss wanted to talk to her. She'd indicated that no one took her claim of a serial killer seriously. Was her presence here unsanctioned?

He wasn't sure if he was on board with the whole serial-killer angle either but he did have a dead body to contend with.

To the men, he said, "Call me when you know anything. I'm taking Special Agent Bennett to headquarters."

At Sami's questioning look, he added, "You can call your boss from there. The IBETs team works out of the consulate general's building on West Pender Street here in Vancouver. The consul general along with US Homeland Security provide oversight for IBETs as well as other binational interagency task forces."

"So I was right. You are working together as a joint team," she murmured, her gaze raking over the men.

"Yes. We're part of the Integrated Border Enforcement Teams—IBETs. There are several such task forces across the shared border between our two countries. Need to keep everyone safe, eh?"

A faint smile touched her lips. "Yes, I'm aware. Can I have my gun and ID back?"

Blake removed the Glock he'd tucked into the waistband of his jeans. "Here you go, princess."

Her lip curled.

Drew suppressed a smile, though he didn't condone the rudeness of his fellow team member. Blake handed over her ID and Drew gestured for Sami to follow him to where he'd stashed his vehicle. "This way."

He opened the passenger door to his twenty-year-old Land Cruiser.

"Sweet ride," she said as she slid inside.

He wasn't into fancy and new. "I like vintage."

When he climbed into the driver's seat, she said, "I have a 1964 Chevrolet Corvair convertible that was my father's. It runs but needs an overhaul. One of these days I'll have the car restored."

"Nice. What color?"

"Baby blue."

Like her eyes. "Pretty."

"It was Dad's pride and joy back in the day."

He didn't miss the note of pride and affection in her tone. "Where's he now?"

"He and Mom live in Seaside, Oregon."

"Your hometown?"

"Yep. Born and raised Oregonian." She described the beachside town in great detail while drumming her fingers on her knee. He sensed her monologue stemmed from nervous energy. Her words made him curious enough to want to visit the ocean town. If only to see it the way she did. She obviously loved her parents and the community she grew up in.

When she fell silent, he asked, "How did you decide to become a federal agent?"

She didn't immediately answer. As the silence stretched, he figured she wasn't going to respond. Then she said, "I have this deep-seated need to see justice done."

Her answer resonated within him. He, too, felt the same drive. He slanted her a glance. Her face was turned away, and she stared out at the passing city. A clear signal that she was done with the conversation. He decided to honor the unspoken request.

When they arrived at the consulate building, Drew parked in his usual spot. They entered the skyscraper and took the elevator to the fifth floor. Drew ushered Sami to the IBETs offices. Few lights glowed in the quiet building. The cubicles and offices were empty. In the corner office where he had his desk, he gestured for her to take a seat in one of the two red upholstered chairs facing the desk. "You can use the desk phone to call your boss."

She didn't sit. Instead she produced a cell phone from one of her pants pockets. "I'll step out into the hall."

Nodding, he rounded the large oak desk to sit in the leather captain's chair. "I'll take you to your hotel after I write my report." And put her on the next plane back to the United States. He couldn't have her running around messing up any more operations.

He watched her silently leave the office, her back straight, her chin level. He wondered what shade of blond her hair was underneath the dark stocking cap. Giving himself a mental shake, he opened an email window and copied the people in charge of the IBETs program—the consulate general, the deputy director for US Homeland Security and the RCMP deputy commissioner of federal policing.

He quickly detailed the events of the evening, as well as his assessment that there might be a potential serial killer on the loose but that he had to do further research before moving on this information. He wasn't ready to buy into Sami's claim yet, despite the sincerity of the pretty agent.

"You are supposed to be on vacation, Agent Bennett." Special Agent in Charge Rob Granger's voice boomed into Sami's ear. "Why are you in Vancouver, interloping on an IBETs investigation?"

Sami rubbed the bridge of her nose with her free hand while she stood in the hallway a few feet from Drew's office. The carpet beneath her feet had a dizzying geometric pattern that added to the headache brewing behind her eyes.

She turned her back to Drew's open door while she quickly explained to her boss her theory that Birdman had set her up. "There was no drug deal going down. It was a trap."

"If that is true, Agent Bennett, all the more reason for you to back off."

"Sir, he's escalating." She told him about the credit card. "Something has changed. If I stop now, how many more people will die? I can't let this go."

Granger's voice dropped. "You're a good agent, Samantha. With a promising career ahead of you. I would hate to see you throw all that away on a personal vendetta."

"This isn't a vendetta." Personal, yes. Lisa was like a sister. But Sami wanted to see justice done, as she'd told Drew. She didn't want any more lives lost. "Sir, please, let me follow the clues where they lead."

"You really do believe there's a case here?"

"I do, sir. And it's within the purview of our office."

"Then we need to assemble a team. Get a profiler involved. Go through the proper protocol. I'll contact the Legat there in Vancouver and get the ball rolling."

The FBI had sub offices located in various parts of the world. The Legats—legal attachés—liaison with the governing authorities. Canada had three sub offices operating in Vancouver, Toronto and the main sub office in Ottawa. Though Sami would appreciate any help they could provide it would take time. Time that James Clark might not have. Or the next victim and the next.

"That sounds great, sir, but in the meantime this unidentified subject is free to continue to kill." Why didn't he understand that she needed to move now, not wait for an official task force to be formed? "Sir, I'm close. I can feel it."

He heaved a sigh. She could picture him rubbing a hand over his jaw the way he did when he was faced with a decision. She sent up a quick prayer he would see the logic in her request. She liked and respected her boss. He and his family were good people.

"I suppose what you do on your own time is none of my business." He paused, then added, "Until it is."

She smiled and leaned back against the hallway wall. "I have two weeks of vacation time accumulated."

"Indeed. I'm giving you some leeway, Agent Bennett. As long as you are an agent of the FBI, you will act accordingly. Check in with the local police and keep me apprised of any and all developments at all times. That means you don't act until you've talked to me. Follow, survey, observe. Gather information. Do I make myself clear?"

"Yes, sir. Thank you, sir."

"I hope I won't regret this, Agent Bennett."

"You won't, sir."

"Don't do anything stupid, Samantha. If you so much as get a whiff of danger, call for backup. Tonight could have gone horribly wrong."

Her insides twisted with the truth of his words. "Yes, sir."

After hanging up, Sami found the restroom, where she rinsed her face with cold water. The white tiled sink and chrome faucet gleamed in the overhead fluorescent lights. A large rectangular mirror covered the wall behind the sink and her reflection stared back at her.

Tonight could have gone horribly wrong.

The words rang through her head. If Drew hadn't stopped her from entering that motel room, what would have happened?

But he had and now she was in the Canadian Consulate General's headquarters. A place she'd never imagined she'd end up tonight. But then again, she hadn't known what to expect. Certainly not being detained by a handsome Canuck with control issues.

Her hands shook. A normal response given the adrenaline letdown. She needed to pull herself together.

But the frustration from not catching Birdman tightened her shoulder muscles. She should have been used to disappointment by now, but pessimism wasn't normally her bag. Lisa would say Sami was a discouraged optimist. An oxymoron for sure.

A knock on the door startled her. Her hand went to her holstered gun. "Yes?"

"I'm finished with my report. Are you ready?" Drew's muffled voice eased the spike of anxiety.

"Be right out," she called.

She removed her stocking cap and let her hair fall to her shoulders. She finger combed the long strands as best she could then tied them back with a scrunchie she'd found in a pocket. She pinched her cheeks to give her face some color, but the dark circles of fatigue rimming her eyes were a lost cause. What did it matter, anyway? She wasn't trying to impress Drew.

She stuffed the cap into her pocket before opening the door. Drew stood with one shoulder propped against the wall, his tall, lean frame relaxed. Handsome. The thought invaded her mind. The man was definitely good-looking, even with the signs of fatigue around his eyes and the day's growth of beard shadowing his strong jawline.

He'd changed into navy khakis and a collared shirt beneath a jacket with the letters RCMP on the breast pocket, and on the back, as she'd seen earlier. Like hers. Only she had no jurisdiction here.

Despite her badge, at the moment she wasn't acting as an agent of the United States but as a woman obsessed with finding a killer who'd murdered her best friend.

Drew pushed away from the wall. "Where are you staying?"

She gave him the name of a popular hotel chain in downtown Vancouver, then followed him to his vehicle where she settled into the passenger seat and let her curiosity about the man driving prompt her to ask, "How long have you been with the RCMP?"

"I was born into it," he said with a grin.

She made a face. "What?"

"My dad's a retired Mountie. For as long as I can remember, I've wanted to follow in his footsteps."

She wondered what Drew had been like as a kid. A strange tenderness filled her as she imagined a dark-haired boy hero-worshipping his father.

For the next ten minutes they chatted, keeping the conversation light and discovering similar tastes in movies and book genres. Drew followed the National Hockey League, while she could recite pro-football stats. She found him to be engaging and easy to be with. Strange considering their meeting. She'd have guessed they wouldn't find so much to talk about. But when it came right down to it, they were more alike than was comfortable but for some reason she didn't mind.

Drew pulled up in front of her hotel. Sami opened her door, grateful that for a few minutes she'd let herself be normal and been able to push thoughts of Birdman to the back burner. She had this man to thank. He'd made it easy to take a moment to breathe before she rushed back into her investigation. "Thank you for… well, everything."

"My pleasure, Sami."

When Drew turned off the engine, tension rushed into tight a knot in her tummy. It was one thing to let down her guard for the drive over but another completely for him to come to her hotel room door. "You don't have to walk me up."

"I don't have to but it's the polite thing to do." He climbed from the vehicle before she could protest further.

Nerves on the edge of snapping, she decided not to fight him on this. She wanted to hang on to the last remnants of peace in the hope she might sleep tonight. She'd heard Canadians were super polite and friendly. He was living up to the reputation.

The doorman opened the glass door to allow them entrance. Sami smiled her thanks. Soft classical music played in the lobby. The polished marble floors gleamed and teakwood accents added texture, while plush, comfortable seating arrangements invited private conversations.

After nodding a greeting to the concierge, they took the elevator to the second floor. She slid her electronic key in the lock, waited for the green light, then pushed open the door. Darkness lay within.

Confusion made her hesitate. The overspill of the

hallway light reached a few feet in front of her. She frowned and hovered on the threshold.

Drew stepped close, so close she could feel the heat from his body battling the sudden chill chasing down her spine. "Something wrong?"

"I left a light on when I headed out."

"Most likely the maid turned it off after cleaning your room."

Though that sounded plausible, the need for caution didn't ease. She stepped inside the room and groped the wall for the light switch. When she flipped it, nothing happened. Her stomach knotted. She withdrew her sidearm.

Drew's hand on her shoulder gently nudged her aside so he could step past her and move farther into the darkened room. Normally, she'd balk if a man took the lead away from her. She wouldn't let anyone view her as less because she was a woman. But since she had no jurisdiction here and, frankly, was a little freaked out, she allowed him to enter first.

The curtains were drawn; however, a little light from the parking lot outside slipped through the edges, enough to cast gray shadows. Sami's breathing slowed as she strained to listen. Was someone in the room?

She followed Drew deeper into the gloom. Heard him try the table lamp. But the room remained dark.

When she felt the air move, she whipped toward her left. A hissing sound filled her head and something hit her in the face, stinging her eyes, her nose, her mouth.

Pepper spray!

She gagged and spit. Fear fisted in her chest.

Drew's guttural growl said he, too, had been squirted with the offending substance.

They were both vulnerable and the thought terrified her.

Suddenly, the floor-length curtains on the other side of the room were yanked aside. Light from the hotel's back parking lot filled the room. Sami blinked back the tears of stinging pain. She could make out a dark figure at the patio door. She raised her gun but the intruder slid open the glass door and escaped over the balcony and into the night before she could sight down the barrel.

Drew gave chase, disappearing behind the assailant.

She stumbled forward intent on pursuit but she made it only to the sliding door before Drew returned.

He wiped his eyes with the sleeve of his jacket and growled, "I couldn't see which way he went."

A sense of urgency gripped her. "Come on—we need to wash this stuff off." She groped for his hand and latched on to lead him to the bathroom.

Thankfully, the light in the bathroom worked. She turned the cold water on, grabbed two washcloths from the rack and drenched them before handing one to Drew and using one herself.

After a few minutes the burning from the pepper spray was relatively under control. Drew found a pile of lightbulbs on the bed. He screwed one into the table lamp and turned it on. The warm glow expelled the shadows.

Sami's gaze caught on the wall above the king-size bed. Her heart slammed into her ribs so hard she put a hand over her chest to protect herself.

Drew's shocked hiss echoed in the stillness of the room.

Her mouth went dry.

WATCHING YOU

The words were scrawled in bright red letters on the beige-colored wall.

She gasped for breath, but her lungs refused to cooperate. Dark spots danced at the edges of her mind. She fought for control, hating the violated and vulnerable feeling invading her. Only one other time in her life had she felt this way and she'd vowed to never be a victim again. "No!"

So much for her vow or her determination. This situation was out of her control. She mentally scoffed. Of course she wasn't in control. Only God was. Her fingers curled into fists. But where was God when Lisa was being murdered?

Forcing back the searing question, she concentrated on the current situation.

Birdman had been here. In her room. The sense of violation permeated through her like a virus, making her stomach roll.

"How did he find out where I was staying?" Her shaky voice echoed in the silent room. "I let him slip away again!"

And now the hunter had become the hunted.

With a lump of rage lodged in his chest at being caught unaware, Drew called hotel security. He wanted to view their video surveillance. He needed to catch a glimpse of the killer because he hadn't caught sight of the perpetrator's face before he'd vanished in the dark like a wisp of smoke.

No go.

Unfortunately, the security system had suffered a power failure and they were working on getting it back online. Coincidence? Not likely. This killer was savvy enough to down a sophisticated security system. Of course he'd knock out the hotel's video surveillance before infiltrating Sami's room.

Drew's nerves jumped to think what would have happened had he not walked Sami to her room.

What was the guy's plan? To pepper spray her and then…kill her or kidnap her?

Either way, Drew wasn't going to let the guy have another chance.

"Pack your bags," he said.

She turned from inspecting the writing on the wall. "This is paint, not blood."

"The crime scene technicians can try to find a match to the color and brand and see who bought some recently." He picked her suitcase up off the floor and put it on the bed. "I need to take you someplace safe."

Pensive, she nodded and retrieved her clothing from the drawers and the closet. Once she had everything stowed in the suitcase, he grabbed the bag and urged her out of the room just as the local authorities arrived. He ran down the incident. He didn't expect them to find prints; the guy had worn gloves. That much Drew had seen.

"Where are we going?" Sami asked minutes later as they settled in his Land Cruiser.

Good question. There was only one safe place he could think of on short notice. "My place."

THREE

"Are you sure this isn't an inconvenience?" Sami asked. She didn't feel right about intruding on his personal life.

"Not at all."

She followed Drew up the walkway of a well-lit two-story house at the end of a quiet tree-lined street on Vancouver's east side. Fancy sconces were mounted on either side of the rust-colored front door. The house itself was painted a pale yellow with white trim. Empty window boxes created a lonely feeling in the pit of Sami's stomach.

He unlocked the door and walked inside, flipping lights on as he went. She came in behind him and closed and relocked the door.

The house was silent and smelled faintly of savory pasta sauce. Sami's stomach grumbled loudly. Embarrassed, she placed a hand over her tummy.

Drew's chuckle heated her face. "I'm hungry, too." He set her bag by the foot of the staircase. "I'll make us some eggs and toast."

He led her through the house toward the kitchen.

The living room had well-worn hardwood floors and

brown leather furniture placed strategically in front of a large plasma television, making her wish this were a lazy Sunday afternoon and they were here to watch football.

A much better reason for invading his space than hiding from a madman.

On one wall, a floor-to-ceiling brick fireplace with a stack of wood piled in the firebox behind an ornate glass screen made her think of hot chocolate and cozy winter nights. Over the mantel hung a black-and-white landscape of a windy river cutting through snowy peaks and wooded lands. She recognized the style of a popular American photographer. The place was homey and inviting yet masculine. A bachelor pad.

No signs of flowers or any frilly things to suggest a woman's touch. She slanted Drew a quick glance. She'd noticed the absence of a ring on his left hand. Did that mean he wasn't attached, or did he just not wear a wedding ring while on the job?

Better to ask and appease her curiosity than let the question fester. "Your wife won't mind me being here?"

He flipped on the overhead light in the kitchen. The '70s-style mustard-colored Formica countertops were clean. A cast-iron skillet hung from a hook over the gas stove. "I'm not married."

She wasn't sure why she felt relief. His marital status had nothing to do with her. Yet she was itching to ask him why he wasn't married. He was good-looking, employed and had a great personality. All the things any sane woman would be crazy not to pursue. But she didn't want to let things get personal. She mentally snorted. As if staying in his guest room weren't personal.

He glanced over his shoulder. "Are you married?"

She met his gaze. "No."

"Why not?"

Her mouth twisted. He apparently had no problem asking the question. She went with the less complicated answer. "No time for romance."

"Ah. I can relate to that." Drew opened the mustard-colored refrigerator and took out a carton of eggs and a loaf of bread.

From his tone it sounded as if he meant no time for romance was also the reason he wasn't married. Whatever his reasons, they were his. She wasn't crazy enough to delve into the whys and whatnots.

Spying the toaster, she took the bread from him. "You concentrate on the eggs. I'll be the toast master."

He grinned. "I like your way of thinking."

She liked him. Which was surprising considering earlier tonight he'd derailed her plans of capturing Birdman, but then again, as she'd concluded earlier, he'd saved her life. Twice now. An endearing fact, one she'd have to remember to keep in perspective. They shared the same commitment to their respective jobs. And that included saving a fellow law enforcement agent from harm.

She put two slices of bread in the toaster slots. As she twisted the tie on the end of the plastic bag, she was reminded of being tied up not so many hours ago. Thankfully, her wrists bore no marks from the zip ties.

A thump overhead sent a jolt of alarm through her body and kick-started her heart. She dropped the loaf of bread and reached for her weapon.

"Whoa, stand down," Drew said softly.

Her gaze swung to him. "Did you hear that? Someone's in your house."

"It's my dad." He covered her hand holding the gun with his. The warm pressure sent tingles up her arm. His hands were big, strong and capable. "You're safe here."

The way he looked at her, as if he was really concerned for her, made her want to believe him. For some reason this man inspired trust.

Heavy footfalls sounded on the wooden staircase. An older man, wearing a white T-shirt and flannel pants, stepped into the kitchen and halted abruptly. His assessing gaze was cool as he regarded Sami and her gun, then swung his gaze to Drew. "I take it we have a guest, eh?"

"Yes, Dad." Drew removed his hand from over hers. "We have a guest. This is Special Agent Sami Bennett of the FBI. Sami, my dad, retired RCMP inspector Patrick Kelley."

Exhaling, Sami quickly released the hold she had on her weapon before thrusting out her hand at Drew's father. "Nice to meet you, sir."

Warily, Patrick slid his big hand into hers. His calloused palm scraped against her skin. She could see the resemblance between father and son. Both were tall and formidable with the same dark hair and hazel eyes. Drew's face had more angles and planes, whereas the elder Kelley's face was softer and lined with age.

"Likewise, Sami." Patrick shook her hand briefly. "It's not often I enter my kitchen to find a beautiful woman holding a gun. Special agent, eh?"

Heat rushed to her cheeks at the compliment and for the fact she'd almost drawn on him. "I'm sorry about that. It's been a stressful night."

"Eggs, Dad?" Drew went back to scrambling eggs in a bowl.

"Don't mind if I do, eh?" Patrick bent down to pick up the loaf of bread. "I'll have some toast, as well."

Sami cringed at the result of her embarrassing reaction. "Here, sir, let me."

He handed over the bread and then turned to retrieve plates from the cupboard. "So, Sami, what brings the FBI to our door?"

"A case." She pushed down the toaster button and sneaked a glance at Drew. How much would he tell his father?

"How long have you known my son?"

Drew poured the scrambled eggs into a sizzling pan. "We actually met tonight."

Patrick's eyebrows rose. "This I can't wait to hear."

An hour later Drew walked Sami to the guest room at the top of the stairs. He pushed open the door, glad to see the room was made up. They didn't have many visitors, so the room wasn't used often.

"You should find everything you need. Extra blankets and pillows are at the top of the closet." He pointed to the door across the hall. "Restroom's there. Towels and washcloths are in the cupboard under the sink."

Sami gazed up at him. Her blue eyes reflected the hall light, making them glow. "Thank you for everything."

"You're welcome."

She pushed her honey-blond hair over her shoulder. "I like your dad. He's a character."

A strand of her hair stuck to her black sweater. Her hair looked so silky and soft he wanted to touch it. Instead he jammed his hands into his pockets. "Dad was in rare form tonight. He's not normally so chatty."

"I don't mind chatty," she said, her voice soft and breathless.

He met her gaze, noticing the lighter ring of blue around the darker pupils. She had pretty eyes. It had been a long time since he'd felt the pull of attraction the way he did with Sami. His pulse quickened, setting his nerves on edge.

He mentally shut down his reaction. He wasn't looking for a personal relationship with her. Or anyone, for that matter. The last time he'd fallen for a woman, he'd ended up nursing another wound to his battered heart. Not quite as devastating as his mother's abandonment but close enough to make him even more wary.

He took a step back. "Is Sami short for Samantha?"

She gave an imperceptible nod. "My dad calls me Sami."

He liked the nickname, more approachable and feisty, like the woman. "It suits you."

One corner of her mouth lifted, drawing his attention. She had nicely shaped lips. Lips made for kissing. He tugged at the collar of his shirt, suddenly feeling as if they were standing under a heat lamp rather than the soft glow of the hallway light.

"Where's your mom?"

Her question doused the mood like a bucket of ice in his face. What was he thinking? Kissable lips? Silky hair? *Dude, get a grip.*

He needed to stay focused on the objective. Keep Sami safe and find a killer. Nothing more. Nothing less. Attraction had no place in this high-stakes situation.

"That's a discussion for another time, another day." Or never. "Good night, Sami."

Her head tilted to the side with curiosity and…was that disappointment? The awkward silence stretched. The need to open up tugged at him. *Not going to happen. Keep this professional*, he chided himself.

He cleared his throat. "Okay. Good night, then."

The trill of his cell phone echoed through the quiet house. He pulled the device from his pocket. "Inspector Kelley." As he listened to Blake's news, a knot formed in his stomach. "Okay. Tomorrow we'll follow up." He clicked off.

"Well?"

He met Sami's expectant gaze. "The victim was an American woman from Kansas. Melinda Watson. She was in town for a job interview."

Anger and empathy flashed in her blue eyes. "And the credit card? Did they find out anything about the cardholder?"

The knot tightened. "Mr. Clark's a Canadian. He owns an aviation-parts business and is married with two adult kids. His wife told officers that her husband was at a convention in Las Vegas. He had texted her to say he was extending his stay. That was five days ago. She's heard nothing from him since but hadn't panicked, because they were having marital problems and she was thankful for the time away from each other."

"I'm going to Las Vegas. I could catch a flight out tonight."

Drew held up a hand. "Slow down. The card was last used in Phoenix, Arizona, two days ago. Mr. Clark registered at a spa resort."

She gave a sharp nod. "Then I'll go to Arizona. Cloud Jet Airlines has reasonably priced flights."

He marveled at her dedication. She traveled on her own dime. He shook his head. "Which may be what the killer wants you to do."

She shrugged. "I have to catch this guy."

"Why you?"

Pain flashed in her eyes. "He killed my best friend. I won't stop until he's brought to justice."

Compassion flooded his veins. If anyone had hurt someone he cared about, he'd want to do the same thing. But he'd be cautious enough to know taking on a killer by himself wasn't a good idea. He couldn't let her do this alone. The killer had brought his carnage to Drew's door—Drew planned to repay the favor and help Sami capture the man. He'd have to okay it through his boss, but if that didn't fly, then he'd take a lesson from Sami and opt to take some vacation time. "I'm going with you."

Her eyes widened. "I work alone."

"Not anymore."

She tucked in her chin and narrowed her gaze. "As much as I appreciate that you saved my bacon twice tonight, I don't want a partner."

"You don't have a choice. This now involves both of our countries." He could see the protest forming in her eyes. Before she had a chance to speak, he said, "Look, finding and capturing Birdman will go quicker and more smoothly if we combine our resources. There's no reason for you to do this alone anymore."

She pressed her lips together and inhaled, then slowly released her breath. "Fine. Just don't get in my way."

He grinned. He couldn't deny he looked forward to

catching a killer. But he also looked forward to getting to know more about Special Agent Bennett. "I wouldn't dream of it."

The next morning, after a hurried breakfast of toast and coffee, Drew and Sami piled into Dad's car with Dad insisting on driving them to the airport.

"Thanks, Dad. I'll let you know when I'm coming back." Drew shut the door to his dad's luxury sedan and watched as his father pulled away from the curb outside the terminal at the Vancouver International Airport.

Drew had had to hide his surprise at how taken Dad was with Sami. He must be mellowing in his old age. Normally his father was suspicious of women, especially ones Drew showed interest in. Something that didn't occur often these days, because he was still smarting from Gretchen's betrayal.

However, Drew was his father's son, after all, and had suffered the same hurt and heartache as his dad when Colleen Kelley walked out of their lives. And again when Drew's marriage fell apart. But his past had nothing to do with the present. His association with Sami was strictly business. He would keep things professional despite his growing interest in her.

He and Sami checked in with airport security, presenting their IDs, filling out the necessary paperwork and having their weapons inspected. Once they were cleared, they made their way to the gate, where they filed onto the Cloud Jet airplane with the rest of the passengers.

Drew wouldn't have guessed so many people would head willingly to one of the hottest places in the summer. He wasn't looking forward to the heat of Arizona in July.

It had taken some fancy talking on his part to convince his boss the trip was warranted. The deputy commissioner had granted him permission but wanted to be kept apprised of the situation. Not a problem, Drew had assured him. He didn't want to jeopardize his standing with IBETs.

"That's us," Sami said from behind him. "Thirteen A and B."

He moved past their row of seats so she could step in and have the window seat. She set her suitcase on the floor, then opened the overhead compartment. Before Drew could reach for the suitcase, the man coming in behind her picked up the case and tucked it into the luggage space with quick efficiency.

"There you go," the man said with a polite smile.

"Thank you," Sami murmured, and slipped into her seat. Drew nodded his thanks to the stranger, then settled into his seat beside Sami. His knees hit the folddown table attached to the back of the seat in front of him.

In the cramped space, his shoulder and upper arm bumped against Sami. The little sparks each connection created unnerved him. It was hard to stay professional when she set his blood on fire. He shifted away, but short of sitting in the aisle, there was nowhere to go.

As she fiddled with her seat belt, he took in her appearance. She wore a flowery blouse and light-colored cargo pants. She carried no purse today. Her ID and gun were stashed in the deep pockets of her pants, and the knife she'd used to free herself was hidden away. Most likely in a boot. Big and clunky, they were in stark contrast to the feminine top. Yet the ensemble worked for her. Very Portlandian.

Her blond hair was held back by a barrette at the nape of her slender neck and smelled like his shampoo. He could tell she'd applied a touch of mascara to the black lashes framing her pretty eyes, and her lips shone with gloss.

She looked so different from the woman dressed like a ninja last night. However, both sides of the lady appealed to him, despite his need to stay detached emotionally. She was brave and spunky when she needed to be but didn't flaunt those traits as if needing to prove her toughness.

He waited until after takeoff to ask, "Tell me how you became involved in this case. You said your friend was a victim?"

Her lips pressed together for a moment. She nodded. "Lisa and I were like sisters. The Westovers lived next door. Seaside isn't a big community. At least not for those who live there year-round. Our families became close."

"When was Lisa killed?"

"Six months ago. Her case went cold quickly." She told him in graphic detail how similar Lisa's murder was to the crime scene from last night. "Birdman is clever and knows how to not leave behind trace evidence."

"Except for bird drawings and writing on the wall," he remarked drily.

"Done without leaving fibers or DNA."

"How did you connect this Birdman to Lisa's murder?"

She frowned. "I didn't at first. I searched for similar

crimes in the metro Portland area and came up empty. Then I spread out from there via the FBI's ViCAP."

The Violent Criminal Apprehension Program, a searchable database to collect and analyze crime, was the model that the Canadian government followed for their own version, ViCLAS—Violent Crime Linkage System. Both automated systems were invaluable to IBETs and all law enforcement in both countries. "We have something similar."

She gripped the armrests as the plane bounced through turbulence. "I found comparable crimes across the US but never in the same city. By then my boss realized what I was doing and wasn't pleased, despite the fact I was investigating on my own time."

She shrugged. "There wasn't much he could say, though. He definitely wasn't okay with me leaving Portland to investigate crimes outside our field office assignments. But I couldn't stop. I had to know. I had to see if there were any connections to Lisa's murder."

"So this trip to Vancouver...?"

"Technically I'm on vacation. The special agent in charge has given me some rope." Her mouth tipped up at the corners. "Probably enough to hang myself with."

Not if he could help it. She'd been targeted twice now. She obviously wasn't safe alone. Not that he saw her as a damsel in distress. Far from it. She'd shown bravery and smarts. And the drive to do what was necessary to stop a criminal. "Your dedication is admirable."

"Thanks." She shrugged. "I made a promise to Lisa's parents that I'd find her killer. I always keep my promises."

The flight attendant stopped to offer them drinks and the opportunity to purchase a snack from the cart.

They each ordered a drink and a snack plate of fruit, cheese and nuts. While the attendant poured their drinks and handed over their plates, Drew contemplated Sami's statement.

Did she truly honor her promises? Or were her words just that—words?

Gretchen had made promises to love and honor and cherish him. But she'd broken those promises so easily. Drew was wary of any woman's promises.

Once the flight attendant had moved on and they'd opened their refreshments, he said, "I don't know many people who would go to such lengths to pursue justice for their friend."

"I don't know many people who would leave their country to help a stranger pursue justice for her friend."

He mirrored her earlier shrug and collected a small handful of cashews and almonds. "It became my business when we discovered the man we're going to see is Canadian."

Not to mention, Drew had decided to take it upon himself to be Sami's protector. Twice now she could have been killed. Silently he vowed he wasn't going to let that happen. The woman needed help whether she wanted it or not.

"Promise me you'll be careful," she said, her tone intense.

He gave her a half smile. "Careful is my middle name."

He popped a chunk of cheese and an apple slice into his mouth.

"I'm serious. I have enough to contend with bringing down Birdman. I don't need you being a hotshot and taking unnecessary chances."

"Where's this anxious fretting coming from? I'll be careful."

She breathed in and slowly exhaled. "Sorry. I haven't worked with a partner on this." She dropped her gaze and concentrated on her food.

"I see." She was a lone wolf taking down a predator. But not anymore. "Tell me about the bird symbol."

She visibly collected herself, took a drink of her pop. "When I was digging through the various case files I noticed bagged evidence that was incongruent with the crime scenes. Things that had appeared irrelevant or unimportant at the time. No fingerprints, no DNA showed up, so the clues lay dormant in musty files of cold cases. A playing card here. A postcard there."

She drummed her fingers on her knee. "At Lisa's murder scene a business card was found tucked into her handbag. Nothing unusual about that, since she was in sales. Which was why she was staying at the hotel by the airport the night she was killed. She had an early morning flight." Sami's voice broke. "I would have driven her in the morning if she'd only asked."

He covered her hand with his, stilling the nervous drumming. She turned her hand over so their palms met. Her fingers laced through his. He refused to read anything romantic in the gesture. Talking about her friend upset her. He was merely offering the only comfort he could. Holding her hand meant nothing, even if her small hand fit snugly within his as if were made for each other.

"There was a little stamp on the back corner of the business card," she continued, apparently unaware of the turmoil going on inside him. "I didn't think much of it at first. But then I noticed the bird on other pieces of evidence and realized he was leaving his signature."

Keeping his voice low so as not to disturb the other passengers, he said, "And all the women were strangled, and then their bodies were mutilated."

"Yes." She lowered her voice, as well. "He used his hands to crush their larynxes and then desecrated them. He never uses the same knife. Different styles of cutting instruments. No discernible pattern. But there's one thing all the deaths do have in common. The women met their attacker at a hotel or airport bar and restaurant."

"Sexual assault?"

"No. There's no apparent motive for the deaths that I can tell. Only the killer knows what drives him."

"And you're sure it's a male perpetrator?"

"Yes."

"He was caught on camera?"

She gave a mirthless laugh. "Not in any discernible way. He's too savvy for that. Knows where surveillance cameras are located or, like at my hotel, knocks out the system. He never looks the same in what footage I do have. And witness statements run the gamut of short and round to tall and muscular. Blond, dark, ginger. Large nose, crooked nose. Eye color is all over the board."

"So it could be a woman in disguise."

Her keen eyes lit up with a hint of success. "The one thing he didn't think to hide was his hands. Big knuckles, strong hands." She lifted their joined hands between them. "A man's hands."

The guy who'd been in her hotel room had had on

black gloves. "But if he didn't hide his hands then, why were there no prints?"

Her lip curled. "That's the million-dollar question." She shrugged. "I have a few theories. He could have worn thin flesh-colored gloves. He could have dipped his hand in sealant or glue, for that matter." The frustration in her voice was unmistakable.

She extracted her hand from his and turned to stare at the passing clouds outside the window. She was something special, this FBI special agent. He'd never met anyone like her. Courageous and assertive, yet he'd caught glimpses of vulnerability.

Funny how life turned out sometimes. God's sense of humor at work?

Drew had been content with his life after the turmoil of his divorce. He'd made inspector by thirty. He'd been asked to join and then lead an IBETs team. He shared a bachelor pad with his dad and had no plans to change that anytime soon.

He hadn't been looking for a cause or a partner, yet here he was flying south over the United States with a woman on a mission—to stop a serial killer before he struck again.

And Drew couldn't think of anywhere else he'd rather be.

FOUR

Consulting the map app on her phone, Sami read the directions to the spa resort to Drew rather than having the annoying voice of the system direct them. Though if truth be told, Sami liked to be in control and not leave her fate to some technological device. She could look at the map and gauge for herself the most direct route.

She wished she had equal control of the car. Drew drove the rental through the fast and furious Phoenix traffic as if he'd been doing so his whole life, causing her to grasp the door handle more than a few times.

"So, Royal Canadian Mounted Police don't ride horses anymore or wear red-and-black uniforms?" she teased.

He'd be handsome in his uniform. Not that he wasn't handsome in cotton slacks, a white dress shirt and polished Allen Edmonds shoes. He looked more like a banker than a cop. Except for the holster at his waist and the gold badge attached to his belt.

He'd rolled up his shirtsleeves the moment they'd stepped off the plane. She didn't blame him. Over a hundred degrees, the Arizona heat sucked the moisture from her lungs while a sweat broke out on her back and brow.

"The RCMP discontinued using mounted patrol for regular duty in the 1930s," Drew explained. "There is a yearly Musical Ride tour and we wear our uniforms for parades and special events."

"Have you been in the Musical Ride?" She'd like to see him on horseback. There was something about a man on a horse that appealed to her—and every other female. The mystique of the cowboy, she supposed. Or a Mountie, as the case may be.

"No. Horses and I don't mesh well."

She raised an eyebrow, curious if he meant what she thought he meant. "Afraid?"

"Horses are big unpredictable creatures. I'd rather stay on the ground and watch."

"If we have to head out in the desert, you're hoofing it on foot?"

The color drained from his face. "That's not even funny. I can barely tolerate this heat in an air-conditioned car. I don't want to think about the desert."

She laughed, liking that he wasn't afraid to admit to a foible. Not for the first time, she found herself realizing how much she liked this man. He didn't have that macho chip on his shoulder the way so many men did when they discovered she was in law enforcement.

Women's equality might be alive and well; however, she'd faced her fair share of discrimination moving up the ranks of the Bureau. But Drew seemed to genuinely respect her, which she appreciated and in return respected.

Being with him was easy. She didn't have to force conversation or feel as if she needed to prove something to him. He accepted her.

She couldn't remember the last time she'd met some-one and felt an immediate connection.

The thought sent agitated shivers over her sweat-drenched flesh. She wasn't going down any road that led her to losing control of her emotions. Connection or not, she had a job to do. She could appreciate Drew as another professional; she could even appreciate him as a good-looking, charming man. She could handle attraction but nothing else.

He made a left turn into the Majestic Palms Re-sort parking lot. Desert hills, towering palms and spiky cacti surrounded the elegant sprawling salmon-colored mansion-turned-hotel. The grounds of the resort were stunning, with flowering bushes heavy with red blooms, various-sized palm trees with wide and variegated fronds. A beautiful splashing water fountain drew her gaze. She couldn't help but wish this visit were for a more pleasant purpose.

She stepped out of the car. Waves of heat bounc-ing off the pavement hit her in the face like a wake-up slap. There was a purpose to this visit and it wasn't to allow herself to bond with the man at her side. They might be working together for now, but as soon as they found his fellow countryman, dead or alive, she'd send Drew on his way.

Then she could breathe again, because despite his assertion that their combined resources would make quick work of capturing Birdman, as long as they were together, she'd feel responsible for Drew's welfare. She wasn't going to let him get hurt on her watch. She car-ried enough guilt for what had happened to Ian, her last partner, to last a lifetime.

They wound their way on a cobblestone path through wide arches to the resort lobby.

Drew gestured to the two Phoenix police officers waiting discreetly off to the side. Sami squared her shoulders and walked to the office the resort employees directed them to. She'd called the city's chief of police, giving him the pertinent details of their investigation and asking for the local LEOs'—law enforcement officers'—cooperation.

Sami and Drew showed their badges.

"I'm Officer Jensen. This is Officer Grant." The older of the two men made the introductions. "Chief says you need a wellness check on a guest."

"Yes. A James Clark." Drew handed over the fax he'd brought with them. The image showed an average-looking older man of average height with dark hair and dark eyes. "His credit card was found at a crime scene last night. The last charge on the account was here at the bar. A call to Hotel Registration confirmed he was a guest through the weekend. We need you to do a wellness check."

"We have his room number and card key," Officer Grant said. "He has a terrace room on the fourth floor. Room four-oh-six, at the end of the hall."

Adrenaline rushed through Sami's veins. Could Mr. Clark be the killer? Or would they find Mr. Clark's mutilated body?

She and Drew followed the two officers along another cobblestone path to a wing of the resort that stacked to six levels. Each room had a private balcony. The inner rooms overlooked the beautiful courtyard and the reflecting pool that beckoned with its sun-dappled water. The outer rooms, such as James Clark's, had stunning views of the Camelback Mountain in the distance.

They took the stairs to the fourth floor. The hallway was carpeted with swirling greens and rust-colored patterns. The smell of cinnamon overpowered the fragrant scents of the courtyard they'd left behind. The aroma grew stronger as they approached room 406. Though not necessarily an unpleasant smell, it was certainly surprising. Candles? Incense?

A Do Not Disturb sign hung from the doorknob.

Officer Jensen rapped his knuckles on the door. "Mr. Clark? Police. Open up."

No noise emanated from inside the room.

Officer Grant stepped up, knocked again and then slid the key card into the slot. When the green light flashed, he pushed open the door. An intense wave of the spice burned her nose. But beneath the cinnamon scent she detected a foul odor.

All four of them shared ominous glances.

With his hand on his holster, Officer Jensen entered first. "Uh, you guys better get in here."

The officer's dire tone made Sami's heart sink. Most likely Mr. Clark was dead. The certainty took up residence in her chest, squeezing her lungs tight. Steeling herself against the inevitable, she filed into the room behind the men.

She put a finger under her nose but it didn't help quell the nauseating smell. The room was stifling hot. The curtains had been drawn, allowing the sun to bake the inside like a sauna.

Officer Grant clamped a hand over his mouth and ran out of the room. Sami sympathized with the guy.

She suffered with a strong gag reflex and only by sheer force of will was she able to keep from dry-heaving.

Sami's gaze landed on the dead Caucasian woman lying on the edge of the bedspread. She was coated in a white chalky substance that covered her like a dusting of snow. It was hard to determine age. Her dark hair fanned out around her head like a peacock's tail.

"Lime," Drew murmured. A hydrated lime used on farms and in gardens as a soil modifier. When used on a corpse, it delayed the decaying process as well as minimized the stench.

She nodded even as her stomach revolted. She clamped her teeth together to keep from throwing up. Stupid gag reflex. Her personal Achilles' heel.

Give me strength, God, she silently prayed.

On the dresser was an empty bottle of cinnamon oil. The floor was soaked with the liquid spice.

"I take it this is not James Clark," Officer Jensen said. He cleared his throat. "Any chance this Clark fella could be your killer?"

Sami snorted. "No way would it be that easy."

"Too bad." Officer Jensen walked to the open door. "Hey, Grant, call in a missing-person alert on James Clark."

They needed to find Mr. Clark before he turned up dead. Time was not his friend. Sami gestured toward the bed. "How quickly can you identify the victim?"

She ached for the family of the deceased woman. Their loved one wouldn't be coming home.

Drew moved to Sami's side. "See any similarities?"

She tore her gaze from the horrific scene before her to search the room, but she didn't see anything on the desk, the dresser, near the television. She moved into the bathroom. Nothing there either. She didn't understand. Birdman had led her here but now went silent?

When she reentered the bedroom, her gaze fell to the bed. Something stuck out between the mattresses and beneath the body of the unknown woman. The sick madman wanted her close to his handiwork. Fury erupted deep inside her, searing in its intensity. She grabbed a set of thin gloves from her pants pocket and snapped them on.

"I see it," Drew said, apparently reading her intent. "Officer Jensen, Special Agent Bennett is going to remove the paper sticking out from between the mattresses. If you'd be so kind as to have an evidence bag ready."

"Of course." The officer quickly took a bag from his utility belt and held it open.

Bracing herself to confront Birdman's handiwork at eye level, she tugged on the edge of the paper. She swallowed back the rising bile. A brochure slipped out. Officer Jensen swiftly offered the evidence bag for her to drop the long, thin two-sided brochure in. The officer zipped the bag closed and handed it to Drew.

Once the piece was secure, she stripped off the gloves.

"Here." Officer Jensen offered her another evidence bag.

She shoved the soiled gloves inside before shifting her focus to the bag Drew held. "What is it?"

He lifted it up for her to inspect and she took it from him to study the contents. A brochure for a theme park hotel in California. On the back side in the upper left corner was a tiny drawing of a bird.

Birdman's calling card. His signature. Which would lead to another death. And to another clue and another death and another clue…

She rubbed her throbbing temples. Would this nightmare ever cease?

Yes, when the killer was ready. Because right now he had the power and she was dancing to his silent tune like a puppet on a string.

She met Drew's gaze. His hazel eyes hardened to stone. He'd no doubt come to the same conclusion. The killer was getting his jollies from teasing and taunting her. But what choice did she have other than to follow his lead?

Somehow she had to gain control. Shift the balance of power so that she was the one calling the shots. "We have to go to California."

"No."

She stared at Drew. "There's another victim. If I don't find her or him, who will?"

"We'll contact the local authorities. They will take care of the victim." He stepped closer and placed his hands on her upper arms. His warm fingers touched her where the shirtsleeves left her skin exposed. "It's time to stop running after Birdman. We need to get ahead of him."

She wanted that, too. "How do we do that when we don't even know who we're hunting?"

"We start at the beginning." His thumbs rubbed soothing circles on her biceps. "I want to see all the information you've compiled."

She blinked back the burn of sudden tears. For so long she'd been chasing this sicko alone, running on adrenaline and fury. All the while telling herself it was better this way. Better to be alone so there was no chance of anyone else she cared about being hurt.

But now the thought of having someone help shoulder the burden, help make the decisions, eased the tension in her tightly strung nerves. She'd asked God for strength and He was providing Drew. Not what she expected or wanted.

Allowing Drew to be fully a part of the investigation meant putting her life and her promise to avenge her friend's death in his hands. Was she willing to relinquish that much control to him?

She couldn't deny how good it felt to have someone to share this load with. Especially a good-looking, conscientious man such as Drew.

No. She stopped that thought in its tracks. She wouldn't go there. She couldn't let this become personal. She couldn't let her heart become attached to this man. He was in the same business as she was; his job required risk, just as hers did. If he was willing to take on this burden, then she had to stay focused on what was important.

This was about bringing justice to women who didn't deserve to die. She needed to stay dedicated to her goal, stay in control of her emotions. Mixing business with pleasure never ended well.

She'd already made that mistake once and wasn't going to do it again.

However, two smart brains had to be better than the one psychopath.

Who was she to argue with God?

"All right. We go to Portland."

She prayed Birdman wouldn't anticipate that they would return to Portland rather than follow his bread crumbs. Someone else would check the hotel. She didn't envy them the job.

* * *

When they arrived in Portland, Drew was grateful for the more temperate weather. The sky was blue, the sun shining, but the temperature was in the seventies. Sami had parked her small economical car in the airport's three-story parking garage. They left the airport and joined the congested freeway leading into downtown Portland. Drew had never been to the City of Roses before, so he was impressed by the cityscape.

He'd heard of the many bridges crossing the Willamette River, which bisected the city. He counted four before Sami turned off the freeway and wound through a neighborhood she referred to as Hawthorne District, named for the main avenue that ran from the river and traveled east for several blocks. Drew thought the area very avant-garde with trendy shops and coffeehouses. A place he'd like to explore given the chance.

She turned down a residential side street and pulled the car into the single driveway of a quaint-looking home painted a sunny yellow. A well-kept patch of lawn and shrubs provided pleasing curb appeal. Red flowers offered a pop of color in baskets hanging from the porch beams. Sami unlocked the door and walked in.

An eerie sensation of being watched tapped into Drew's consciousness. He glanced behind him, studying the neighborhood for a moment. Cars were parked along both sides of the narrow tree-lined street of the genteel neighborhood. But no one was about in the middle of this Tuesday afternoon.

Shaking off the sensation, he stepped inside the house and immediately noted the built-in gas fireplace and bookshelves that had been painted white and dominated a half wall to his left and a grouping of comfortable-looking furniture in the middle of the living room that provided a cozy conversation area. Recessed windows allowed natural light to fill the house.

"Home, sweet home," Sami said, shutting the door behind him. "I have a spare room upstairs you can use." She led the way toward a staircase.

He followed but halted when he glanced into the dining room. Though a table and chairs stood in the center, his gaze was riveted on the walls, which were covered with photocopies of police reports, newspaper clippings and copies of crime scene photographs, along with DMV-issued photographs of several women.

A large map of North America had been tacked onto a huge piece of corkboard. A colorful array of small pushpins dotted the map.

Unnerved by the pins, he set his suitcase on the floor and moved closer.

"You can see his pattern moving across the US," Sami said, joining him at the board after leaving her suitcase on the bottom stair. She picked up a box of pushpins and added one to Phoenix. She held up another pushpin. "Now he's crossed over the boundary between our countries." She tacked the pin into the little red circle indicating Vancouver.

A shiver of dread chased down his spine. How many more pins on the Canadian side of the map would they have to add to the board?

"I know you said you've been tracking Birdman, but this—" he made a sweeping gesture with his hand to encompass the room "—this has become an obsession for you."

She folded her arms across her chest. Her gaze didn't waver. "Yes. For six months this has been how I occupy my nights and weekends when I'm not working another case."

"Why isn't this an official investigation yet?" She'd told him her boss had wanted to start a case file.

"The FBI only gets involved in local crimes if asked. Each of these murders happened in different jurisdictions. No official request has been made but I've had very good cooperation from the various police agencies. Most police departments are understaffed and overwhelmed."

Impressed and sad at the same time, Drew studied the woman in front of him, noting the lines of stress bracketing her mouth, her eyes. She really was pretty and formidable with the proud tilt to her chin and the squared shoulders. She was ready to take on the world. Ready to take on a killer. Her life had become about hunting death.

A lock of her blond hair had escaped her clip. He reached out to tuck the strands behind her ear. She froze, her breath catching. Instantly the air felt charged with the electricity that sparked between them.

He lowered his hand and stepped back, giving her room and himself space to gather his composure.

What would happen to her when she finally found her friend's killer? Would she have the restraint to not inflict her own brand of justice? Or would she do as her training taught her and apprehend him, letting the courts mete out the justice she fervently sought for her friend and the other victims?

The questions circled in his brain with no answers.

Only time would tell. He prayed she'd find the strength within herself to not seek out revenge but to do the job she'd committed her life to.

FIVE

"Walk me through these crime scenes," Drew said, needing to know what they were up against. She handed him a tall glass of lemonade and set out a plate of cookies on the dining room table before joining him in front of the map and the many signs of Sami's obsession. He needed to hear how she processed all the information she'd gathered.

As she talked, he listened, growing more overwhelmed and appalled with each passing minute. Separately the crimes did appear random. No two were exactly alike. The perpetrator wasn't ritualistic in his approach to killing. That Sami had somehow connected the dots between these crimes spoke to her attention to detail, the trait of a good investigator.

"He seems to be more opportunistic," Sami stated. "Meaning he doesn't stalk these women but rather trolls the bars and restaurants for his victims. And the victims themselves appear random."

She pointed to each photo. "Caucasian, Hispanic, Asian, African-American. He doesn't discriminate based on color or race. Blonde, brunette, black haired. Different occupations. A schoolteacher, a store clerk, a sales professional. There's nothing linking these women together."

"Was each victim found in a hotel room?"

"Yes. These two women." She touched two photographs. One of a pretty brunette in her midtwenties and the other of a striking African-American woman in her thirties. "They were at airport bars but didn't have hotel rooms registered in their names at the hotels they were found in."

Sami tapped the brunette's picture. "Melissa Duncan worked as a flight attendant for an airline. She was last seen in a Boston airport bar having a club soda between flights. When she didn't show up for her shift, the airline contacted the authorities.

"The airport was searched, but she was nowhere to be seen. No one remembers seeing her leave. The airport security video showed her having a drink, then using the women's restroom. But she never came out. Or if she did, the camera missed her exit.

"Her body was found five days later in a hotel room in DC that was registered to—" Sami walked down the line of photos and stopped "—Carol Crosby. Who in turn was discovered two weeks later in a cabin on the outskirts of Tulsa."

"The perp kidnapped Carol Crosby from her hotel and somehow transported her across the country to Oklahoma. That's risky."

"I'm not sure where he abducted Carol from. It could have been the hotel or a nearby location. However, the cabin was a vacation rental that had been rented to Maureen Forbes." She pointed to the photo of a sixty-year-old woman with graying hair. "She was found in a motel in Dayton, Ohio, before Carol's body was discovered."

Drew's gaze darted back to the map. How had the perp moved so easily and so quickly between points?

"Eight deaths that I can confirm as Birdman's because of the bird symbol left at the crime scenes. Or rather nine now with the one in Phoenix. And if there is a murder victim in California who turns out to be his handiwork, then ten."

The scope of the madness boggled his mind.

She moved to stand in front of a photo of a smiling blonde woman. She touched the photo. "Lisa's body was found in a hotel in Chicago. She was supposed to be in Boston. But the last time anyone saw her was in a restaurant at the Portland airport eating a bagel.

"She didn't board her plane. She didn't board any plane that I can find a record of. Yet somehow she got from Portland to Chicago in a shorter amount of time than it would take someone to drive her there."

"What a strange and twisted puzzle." And he could see how she had become obsessed with finding the killer. But he didn't think it was healthy for her to be surrounded by the constant reminders of her friend's murder. "Does your boss know what you're doing? How much time and energy you've put into this?"

"Yes."

"And when this case ends?" Drew asked. "Then what will you do to occupy your time?"

She gave him a sharp glance. "I can't think that far ahead. I need to stay focused on the here and now."

Hence why she had no time for romance, as she'd stated earlier. "Your family must worry about you."

"Yes, they worry. I don't think my dad would have taught me self-defense if he'd known I'd go into law enforcement. But I think my path was inevitable." She walked into the kitchen.

He followed. The kitchen was narrow, with the sink and cupboards along the outside wall, while the big appliances were squished into the corner. "What do you mean?"

She washed her hands at the sink. "When I was eight, my mother and I were held hostage during a bank robbery." As she spoke, she made a salad—ripping lettuce leaves, chopping carrots, crumbling feta cheese, tossing it all with a vinaigrette dressing. Her hands were steady, her movements economical. "One of the robbers grabbed me, using me as shield when the police arrived."

He leaned against the counter. He couldn't believe how calm she sounded. Only the slight pursing of her lips tipped him off that she wasn't as detached as she wanted him to believe. His heart ached with the thought of how young she'd been and what could have happened. "That must have been terrifying."

"It was. The stuff of nightmares." She retrieved two small plates. "Can you get two forks out of that drawer?" She gestured to the drawer he blocked.

He grabbed the forks. "That experience prompted you to join the FBI?"

"That and my father teaching me how to shoot." She smiled with obvious affection for her father. "He was a proficient marksman during his army days. In college I studied criminal justice. I was thinking more along the lines of judge than agent, except the thought of law school didn't appeal. So I applied to the academy and was accepted."

"I'm sure he's proud of you." He dug into the salad

with relish. The dressing was mild and tasty, the lettuce fresh and the cheese salty on his tongue.

After a few moments of silence, she pointed her fork at him. "Tell me about your mother."

He nearly choked on the bite of food in his mouth. He swallowed. Centering himself, he said, "She left my dad and me when I was twelve."

Empathy tinged her blue eyes. "That's rough."

"Yes, well, we did okay."

"Do you talk to her?"

"Occasionally she'll call. But for the most part, no. She walked out on us. There hasn't been much to say."

Sami leveled him with a pointed look. "She's your mother. Give her some grace."

He huffed out a frustrated breath. "Easier said than done."

"You haven't forgiven her."

His gaze dropped to the remains of his salad. "I try. I've prayed but when I think of the way she destroyed our family, all I feel is anger."

Sami curled her fingers over his. Her touch was soft and warm and made tenderness swell within his heart.

"I feel the same about Lisa's death. I don't want to blame God but I get so angry—" She licked her lips.

The need to lean toward her and kiss her punched him in the gut like a physical blow. He swallowed back the lump in his throat. "I guess we both need to figure out how to forgive and let go."

She nodded.

Sami's cell phone rang. She pulled her hand away to fish the device out of her pants pocket. "Agent Bennett."

Her face paled as she listened. "Did you find anything at the scene that seemed out of place?"

"A matchbook," she said, clearly repeating what she'd been told. "Was anything written on it?" She closed her eyes and took a breath. "I see. I'd like a copy of the police file sent to the FBI office in Portland, Oregon." She gave the caller a fax number.

She hung up. "They did find another victim at the hotel in California. Female. Strangled with a pair of nylons. The body was defaced like the others, this time with what they believe to be an ice pick. The medical examiner estimates she's been dead for at least forty-eight hours."

Drew's heart sank.

"The matchbook found at the scene was from a hotel in Victoria, BC. The Grand Hotel. A yellow bird was stamped on the inside cover with the number twenty-three."

Fury burned in his gut. The killer was leading them back across the international border. "I'll call the Victoria PD."

"I need to go there now." Sami moved past him.

He caught her by the elbow. The feral, almost haunted look in her eyes worried him. "It will take us too long to get there. If Birdman is there, our best option is to send in the local police. They can roll within minutes."

"I hate not doing anything," she said. "He's out there killing and taunting me because I'm the one who noticed the murders were connected. What possible motive does he have for murdering these women? For killing Lisa, who was the sweetest, most caring person I've ever known?"

Sympathy stirred tenderness in him. "We won't know until we catch him. We have to have faith that we will."

Her lips twisted with doubt and she shook off his hand. "Easier said than done." She repeated his words back to him.

Allowing her space, he took out his cell phone and called the Victoria Police Department to explain the situation. He requested that officers be sent to the hotel as quickly as possible.

"They'll call back," he assured Sami after he hung up.

She nodded. "I have to be missing something." She walked into the dining room. "There has to be a clue here that I've overlooked."

This was taking a toll on her, eating away at her. He doubted she'd overlooked anything but he'd give everything a second glance. "Do you have the autopsy reports for each victim?"

Glancing at him, she shook her head. "I don't have copies but I have spoken to each medical examiner."

"I'm just wondering if any of the women had defensive wounds."

Sami sighed. "I'd thought of that, too. Especially with Lisa. She was a fighter. But there was no bruising on her hands to indicate she'd fought back. No DNA under her fingernails."

"Tox screens?"

"He used chloroform. The medical examiner believes our unidentified subject makes his own batch to use for drugging his victims because the ratio between chemicals has been inconsistent. Apparently, chloroform can be made with bleach and alcohol. So not only does it knock the victim out, the mixture burns the skin and membranes of the nose. Not that our killer cares. He then somehow transported them to the kill spot."

Drew turned to the map again. "What do all the cities have in common?"

Sami joined him. "Highways. Airports. Tourist trade. Hotels."

"Okay," he said. "Who would most likely travel easily through these cities?"

"Business travelers," Sami said.

"But would a business traveler have the means to transport an unconscious woman from place to place?"

"Hmm. How about truck drivers? We see a lot of illegal immigrants coming across the southern border trapped inside cargo trucks."

"True. But the timing wouldn't work. Right? A truck is a slow way to go. He needs to move his victims from point A to point B rapidly."

"He found several of his victims at airports," she started to say.

He swiped a hand through his hair. "Our unidentified subject could work at an airport, say as a baggage handler. He targets a victim, renders them unconscious and somehow puts them in the cargo area of a plane. Then someone on the other end receives the victim?"

Sami shook her head. "That would mean there was a team of murdering baggage handlers working together. I don't buy that."

"Yeah, that's a bit far-fetched."

The landline rang. Sami went into the kitchen to answer the call. "Hello?"

"There's a surprise for you in your bedroom," the breathy voice whispered in her ear.

A shudder of fear worked over her flesh. "Who is this?"

The line went dead. Sami dropped the phone and swallowed back the panic clawing its way up her throat.

Drew stood in the doorway. "Sami?"

She reached for her weapon. "The killer. He said there's a surprise for me upstairs."

Unholstering his sidearm, he beckoned her to him. She nodded with grim determination. Together they made their way up the narrow stairwell leading to the second floor of her little home. The sense of violation crowding her chest unleashed rage that heated her skin. At the top of the landing, she motioned toward the right and led the way to her bedroom, grateful to not be alone.

Sun poured in through the overhead skylights. Her dresser and nightstand were undisturbed. But the rose-colored wall behind her bed had been defaced with a crudely drawn bird, the same bird that Birdman left as his signature. The red paint—blood?—dripped down the wall.

Her gaze fell to her pillow.

An ear.

She spun away. The irony of the offending gift he'd left on her bed was clear. Birdman had been listening.

Was he still in the house?

She dropped to the floor and checked under the bed while Drew opened the closet. Nothing.

There were two more rooms on this floor. The bath and the guest room.

Leading with her gun, she made her way out of her bedroom. At the bathroom she took a position on one side of the door while Drew took a position on the other. She pushed open the door and reached in to flip on the light switch. Drew entered, checked the shower and returned a second later to mouth, *Clear*.

She nodded and pointed. The door to the guest room was ajar. With two fingers she gestured for Drew to take a position on the right side of the door, while she took the left. He toed the door open all the way. They entered but the room was empty.

"He was here," she ground out in a harsh whisper. "Could he still be?"

Drew stared down the stairwell. He didn't have to answer; she could read his expression. Her stomach churned. While they'd been in her room, had Birdman slipped downstairs? Was he waiting to pick them off as they descended? Or was he long gone and they were chasing their own fear?

Her instincts clamored for caution. With Birdman anything was possible.

Drew moved first, slowly going down the staircase with his gun ready. Sami followed suit. At the bottom of the stairs, they peeled off. She went toward the kitchen, while he moved into the living room.

She opened the pantry. No one lurked among her dry goods. The back door was closed but the lock wasn't engaged. She opened the door and went out to her small backyard. Her patio furniture appeared undisturbed. She checked both sides of the house and came up empty. She went back inside.

"Clear," she called out as she made her way to Drew.

"Clear," Drew repeated.

They met at the bottom of the stairs.

"He probably was long gone before we arrived," Drew said. "Do you have an evidence bag?"

She took a bag from her pocket. "Will you…?"

He nodded and took the bag.

Grateful to not have to deal with the "surprise," she said, "Thank you."

While Drew went back upstairs, she used her cell phone to call the FBI field office in Portland.

Keeping her nerves at bay by sheer will, she filled her boss in.

"A forensic team will be there shortly. And we'll see if we can trace where the call to your house phone came from," Special Agent in Charge Rob Granger said. "I want you to come in where we can protect you. It's time to make this an official case."

It would take time they didn't have to assemble a task force now. She had a more pressing issue that needed immediate action. "Sir, I'm working with Inspector Kelley from the RCMP." She moved into the living room. "I'm requesting permission to officially accompany him to Victoria, BC, where I believe the next murder victim will be found."

Her gaze fell on a rectangular package wrapped in brown paper sitting on the coffee table. She hadn't noticed it when they'd arrived. She bent to inspect the parcel and froze.

A tiny yellow bird had been stamped in the right-hand corner.

The hand holding the phone to her ear dropped to her side as various scenarios shuffled through her mind. The box could hold another body part. Or another clue. Or…a bomb.

The last thought caught and held. She backed away from the coffee table toward the front door. "Drew! Hurry! We need to leave now!"

His footsteps thundered down the stairs. "What's happening?"

She grabbed his arm and pulled him out the front door just as there was an explosion.

And her house went up in flames.

SIX

The world exploded in a cacophony of deafening noise, flying debris and flames. Heart slamming against his ribs and alarm flooding his veins, Drew grabbed Sami in a bear hug to shield her from the worst of the blast and dived for the lawn.

They landed with a jarring thud. Her yelp echoed inside his head. Heat from the explosion battered his back. Something sharp jabbed into his torso. He winced and sucked in a shocked breath. Smoke burned his lungs. He coughed, ducking his head closer to the ground for fresher air.

With his ears ringing, it took a moment for him to realize the shrill sound he heard was actually emergency vehicles. No doubt the neighbors were bombarding 911 with calls.

Slowly, he eased off Sami and felt a stinging sensation in his back, but his focus was on her. She lay unmoving on the ground. Blood matted her blond hair near her temple, and her eyes were closed. A whisper of panic sounded in his mind along with an unspoken prayer. *Please, God, let her be okay.*

He checked her pulse. Strong.

A measure of relief allowed him to push aside his panic to assess her injuries. She appeared unburned, and he saw no shrapnel piercing her body. Gently, he brushed aside a clump of hair to reveal a gash on her scalp near her hairline.

"Sami?" He gave her a slight nudge.

Her eyes popped open. She blinked, her gaze clearing. Then she scrambled to a sitting position.

"Whoa, slow down," he advised. "Take it easy. You hit your head."

She reached up to finger the gash and winced. "What happened?"

"Your house exploded."

With a pained groan, she turned to stare at the flaming remains of her little house. "There was a package on the coffee table." Her voice quivered. "It had a drawing of the bird."

Drew rocked back on his heels. "I don't recall seeing a package when I went into the living room."

Which meant Birdman had been in the house when they arrived. He'd left the package when they'd gone upstairs after his phone call. Was the explosive on a timer or remotely activated? Could the killer be watching them now?

Drew scanned the area. Police were already on scene. Two hustled toward them while others blocked off the area with tape and barriers. The sidewalks were crowded with the curious. Homeowners? he wondered. People on foot from the more traveled streets surrounding the block wanting to see what happened? It wasn't every day a house exploded in such a quiet urban neighborhood.

Could one of the many faces staring at them be the man Sami dubbed Birdman?

The first cop to reach them asked, "Are you hurt?"

Pointing to Sami's bleeding head, Drew said, "We'll need paramedics."

"They're on their way," the officer said, pointing toward an ambulance and a fire truck rolling slowly down the street, barely fitting between the rows of parked cars.

Drew kept a hand on Sami's shoulder, preventing her from standing. "Let the paramedics check you out first."

She grunted and sat back down. "Do you still have the evidence from my room?"

He patted the breast pocket of his dress shirt. "Here."

"Good. We need to give it to an officer right away and have them run DNA." She glanced down at his shirt and gasped. "You're bleeding!"

Her small capable hand tugged him sideways. He craned his neck to see what had her upset. A chunk of glass protruded from his back, and crimson blood soaked his white shirt and dripped onto the grass.

The rush of adrenaline had kept his pain sensors on low boil. He met Sami's gaze. "I barely feel it."

Except even as the words left his mouth, the stinging intensified. Apparently, acknowledging the wound gave his pain sensors permission to squawk. He reached back, intending to pull the glass out, but Sami jerked on his arm.

"Oh, no, you don't. Let the paramedics take care of you." She mimicked his words.

He grinned and conceded the point with a nod.

Two paramedics rushed to their side. One attended to Sami's laceration while the other dealt with his wound.

"Sir, we'll need to remove this at the hospital."

That didn't sound promising. He sent up a prayer that no vital organs had been punctured.

Before they left the scene, he passed off the evidence to a police officer. Sami dug her credentials out of a pocket. "Get that to Forensics ASAP and send the results to the Portland FBI field office."

The officer nodded and hurried away with the bag.

Sami rode with Drew in the ambulance. He lay on his side, facing her while one paramedic stabilized the hunk of glass.

"I'm going to give you a mild pain reliever," the EMT said. Drew felt the pinch of a needle, then a slow-spreading numbness across his back.

As the vehicle rolled away, Drew took Sami's hand. "I'm sorry about the loss of your home."

She squeezed his hand. Tears formed in her eyes. "Me, too. I liked that house." She heaved a heavy sigh. "But it's only things. And things I can replace. We survived."

Her reaction surprised and impressed him. "Most people wouldn't be so cavalier about their possessions going up in smoke." He wondered if he'd feel the same if he lost his home. All the photos and mementos and memories. Some good, some bad.

"Believe me, I'm furious and sad and every emotion you could possibly name." Her voice shook with the intensity of her feelings. "But I can't undo what's done. I hate that he did this. I hate that he invaded my home. I hate that he's trying to destroy my life. But what's that saying—you can't take it with you?"

She shrugged. "Relationships, especially one with God, are more important than material possessions. That's something Birdman will never grasp." A fat tear rolled down her cheek. "There are days when my faith is tested to the brink."

His heart ached for the pain she suffered. "I agree with you that it's hard to be in our line of work and not have our faith waver when we deal with so much evil."

A small smile touched her lips. "Exactly."

He was suddenly gripped by the urge to bury his hands in her hair, pull her close and see if her lips were as soft as they looked. Deliberately, he concentrated on the pain in his back to chase the longing away.

Once he regained his composure, he said, "And you're right—relationships are more important than material possessions."

If only his mother and Gretchen had believed that. Being betrayed by the two people whose love and commitment he shouldn't have had to question had left him wary of ever fully trusting again.

Another thought struck him and he grimaced. "All your research is gone. All your hard work and energy destroyed. Birdman's intent, no doubt."

"Probably. But he's not as clever as he thinks. I have copies of everything in a safe-deposit box."

"Amazing foresight on your part." Respect for this astonishing woman blossomed within him. "Were you anticipating something like this?"

"No. But I had an instructor at Quantico who always made a point of duplicating his files and keeping them off-site, so to speak. He was old-school. I respected him and the idea of always having a backup copy appealed to me."

And she appealed to Drew. She was smart and brave. He liked how her mind worked. He couldn't have asked for anyone better as a partner in the field.

Partner only, he reminded himself. A partner on a case. Nothing more, nothing less.

At the hospital, the ER doctor removed the piece of Sami's front window from his back and stitched up the gash. He instructed Drew to change the bandage often and gave him a couple of pain pills to take until he could fill a prescription. Drew had no intention of impairing his judgment with the pills, so he wrapped them in a tissue and slipped them in his pants pocket.

When he left the exam room, he found Sami in the waiting area sitting on a hard plastic chair in a long line of similar chairs. In the corner a television blared the news, showing the charred remains of Sami's house.

She was talking with an older man wearing a gray striped suit. Her light-colored cargo pants had grass stains, and soot smudged her blouse. Her hair had been tied back with a rubber band and a white bandage covered the cut on her scalp.

As Drew approached, Sami broke off the conversation, stood and studied him. All signs of her tears were gone; in their place was determination. "You okay?"

Glad to see she was back to her feisty self, he nodded. "Five stitches. Thankfully, the glass didn't puncture any vital organs."

Relief flashed in her blue eyes. She touched the bandage on her head. "Two butterfly stitches." She gestured to the man and made the introductions. "Drew, this is special agent in charge of the Portland FBI office Rob Granger."

Ah, her boss. Drew shook the man's hand. "Sir, nice to meet you."

Granger's lips pressed into a grim line. "I wish it were under better circumstances, Inspector Kelley. Thankfully, you both walked away from the explosion with your lives."

"Yes, that is something to be grateful for," Drew agreed. He sent up silent praise to God for the favor of His protection.

"The FBI forensic team is on the scene as we speak," Granger said. "I've been in contact with Deputy Director Moore from Homeland Security, who in turn has been in contact with your consulate general." Drew had never met Director Moore, who called the shots on the American side of IBETs. "We've agreed to a joint operation with the RCMP and FBI, as well as IBETs, utilizing our combined resources to find and capture this man."

With that much manpower behind them, taking down the perp Sami had been chasing on her own should be a piece of cake. Though somehow Drew had an unsettled suspicion that underestimating their prey wouldn't serve them well.

"Birdman," Sami said. "He's slippery. And we don't know when or where he'll strike next. He may have already—like killing the man who owns the credit card we found in Canada."

Drew slanted her a glance. It was unnerving how in tune Sami was to his own thoughts. "Mr. Clark is still missing. I would like to hope he's not dead, but..."

"Doubtful," Sami interjected, clearly anticipating his next words. "We should get his DNA and send it to the forensic team here for comparison."

"Good idea." Drew made a mental note to contact the Toronto local law to have them collect a sample from Mr. Clark's home.

Sami explained their reason to her boss. "Birdman left me a present in my house before the explosion. A body part. We sent it to Forensics for DNA testing. We believe it came from another of Birdman's victims."

Granger inclined his head in agreement. He looked them both over, then removed a notepad and pencil from his pocket and handed them to Sami. "Both of you need to make a list of what you need, clothes and essentials. I'll have Agent Foster bring whatever you need. I booked you rooms at a hotel downtown. Come on—I'll drive you."

They followed Granger out of the hospital to the parking garage. Granger walked a few paces ahead, his long stride eating up the pavement.

Drew's gait was slowed by the pulling of the stitches in his back. The numbing agent fortunately hadn't worn off yet. Sami adjusted her stride to match his. He appreciated her thoughtfulness. She worked on her list as they walked.

Granger reached a black SUV. The beep of the locks disengaging echoed off the garage walls.

The sound of a revving engine reverberated through the stone-and-concrete structure. Tires squealed as a blue sedan shot out from a parking spot ten feet away. The car barreled forward, aiming right at them.

Within Drew adrenaline spiked. With one hand he withdrew his sidearm; with his other hand he shoved Sami at the exact moment she shoved him. Using their combined momentum, they each dived sideways seconds before the car sped past.

Drew grunted as he hit the ground, taking the impact on his shoulder and rolling onto his stomach to protect his back.

A barrage of gunfire split the air as Drew, Sami and

Granger fired at the car. The rear window and taillights exploded.

The car fishtailed before careening out of the parking garage and speeding into the late-afternoon traffic. Angry motorists cut off by the assailant honked as the sedan disappeared from view.

Sami jumped up and ran to his side. Frantic, she grasped his shoulders. "You okay?"

Rolling gingerly to his backside, he grunted as the pain overcame the numbness he'd been so grateful for just moments ago. "Yes." He took her offered hand. "You?"

"Yep." Relief shone in her eyes. She pulled him to his feet.

The stitches protested. He arched as another hiss of pain zipped across his flesh.

Sami put an arm around his waist and moved in close. "You can lean on me."

Though he didn't need a crutch, he couldn't deny how nice it felt to have her pressed so close.

Granger joined them, holstering his weapon. "Did either of you get the plate numbers?"

"I did," Sami said.

"Good." Granger eyed Drew. "We should have the docs recheck your wound."

He grimaced, not wanting to go back inside. He looked at Sami. "Will you check it?"

Her eyes widened at the request. Then she nodded, her expression intent. She lifted his shirt. Her cool fingers probed around the tender edges of the bandage before she gently peeled away a corner. "You didn't pop any stitches and they aren't bleeding."

"Then there's no reason to go back to the emergency room," he said firmly. "Did you see the driver?"

"He had on a baseball cap and sunglasses. The car's visor was pulled down also," she replied after reattaching the bandage and lowering his shirt.

"Yeah, that's what I saw, too."

She moved in close again. "Cliché but effective."

"Couldn't be sure of ethnicity either." He couldn't keep frustration from coating his words. "The guy's bold."

Within minutes the Portland police arrived and took their statements. Sami gave the license number of the sedan to the officers.

Once they were done with the local police, Granger ushered them to the SUV. "Let's get out of here, people."

Drew and Sami slid into the backseat. Leaving the hospital behind, Granger merged the SUV into the afternoon highway traffic.

Drew shifted so that his injured back didn't touch the seat and suppressed a wince. Sami laced her fingers through his. He held on, appreciating her anchoring effect.

"Did the doc give you anything for the pain?" Sami asked, watching him closely.

"He did, but I'm not taking it," he said.

She arched an eyebrow. "Tough guy, huh?"

He shrugged. "Need my brain to be working, not loopy on medication."

"Pain control aids in the healing process."

"You a doctor now, eh?"

"No, but I've been injured."

He shot her a sharp glance. "On the job?"

She lifted her right pant leg to reveal a scar on her

shin. "Bouldering trip up the gorge. A rock and I didn't get along so well."

"I've never been. Rock climbing sounds dangerous."

An impish grin broke out on her face and walloped him in the midsection.

"Maybe someday I'll take you out to Smith Rock," she said. "It's beautiful there. Rivers, hiking trails and rock climbing for all levels of experience."

"You're a risk taker outside of the job, too." He squeezed her hand. "Makes sense considering you've been tracking a killer on your own for six months. A killer that has blown up your house and tried to mow you down."

She grimaced and had the good graces to look a bit sheepish. "Guilty as charged."

But she seemed hardly fazed. He, on the other hand, despised the anxiousness gripping his insides as if he was waiting for the next blow to come. They needed to nail the suspect and put him away. Then Drew would breathe easier.

She lowered her pant leg and then straightened. "Pain causes stress. Stress in turn suppresses the immune system and slows healing."

"I don't think my stress is pain related," he muttered. He had a feeling as long as he was with Sami, he'd be stressed. She challenged him and at the same time she drew him in. The connection forming between them made him uneasy because he was afraid he was harboring more than a professional interest in the beautiful agent.

Letting things get personal between them wasn't a smart idea. Trusting her to have his back was one thing, but trusting her with his heart? Not going to happen.

his cell phone to his ear with one hand and waved her in with the other.

Their rooms were the mirror images of each other. Queen bed, dresser with a plasma TV, a desk and a chair and ottoman near the floor-to-ceiling window overlooking the Portland skyline and the Willamette River with a nice view of Mount Hood in the distance.

Sami entered and sat on the edge of the bed. The pile of replacement bandages that the doctor had sent with Drew lay on the desk. Like a game of charades, she gestured to the bandages and then to his back, hoping he understood her question: Did he want her to change his bandage?

He nodded, still listening to whomever was on the other end of the line.

She quickly opened a new bandage, then stepped up behind him. He smelled like the hotel's sandalwood-scented soap, fresh and clean. Gently, she lifted the hem of his T-shirt and removed the old bandage. The stitches were intact with no blood seeping through, though they were damp from his shower. She wasn't sure he was supposed to have allowed the stitches to get wet yet but since she wasn't his keeper, she kept the thought to herself as she applied a new bandage.

"I appreciate your help," Drew said into the phone. "I'll be in touch."

He clicked off. She stepped away as he turned around. "Thank you."

She smiled. "You're welcome. Though I should be the one thanking you. If you hadn't shielded me from the explosion, I could be the one with the glass in my back."

"I have a feeling you'd have shielded me if I hadn't beat you to it."

She grinned. "Probably."

He held the phone up. "That was the Victoria police. The Grand Hotel is being totally renovated. No guests. They didn't find a victim in or around the hotel."

"This doesn't make sense." Sami turned to stare out the window. The setting sun cast long shadows over the city. Confusion tangled up her thoughts. Fingering the edges of the bandage at her temple, she contemplated this turn of events. "Why plant the hotel matchbook if there's no victim? What if he planned to stash a victim there not knowing the hotel was under construction?"

"That's possible."

She sat on the edge of the bed. "We've lost his trail." Her fingers tapped restlessly on her thigh. "We'll have to wait for another victim." Her voice vibrated with suppressed fury. "Another bread crumb."

He felt the same scalding anger in his chest. "Unfortunately, I think you're right."

"Unless he still plans to go to Victoria. Maybe the clue isn't the hotel itself but the city?" She stood. There was no mistaking the tenacity in her expression. "In the morning we need to head there. Somewhere in the city a body is waiting to be discovered."

SEVEN

The next morning, Drew awoke sore all over his body. Taking a dive onto the pavement had done a number on his shoulder and hip; both areas showed purple bruises. After a dinner from room service, he'd relented and taken one of the pain pills, but the gash in his back had throbbed since the pain medication had worn off in the wee hours of the morning.

He'd been loath to take more. He wasn't sure how long the effects would remain, and the last thing he wanted was to be mentally impaired. Sami needed him coherent and ready to take down Birdman.

Anger at the unknown killer motivated Drew to get up, shower and put back on the fresh clothes bought for him yesterday. He placed a call to his boss with an update of the situation and then made a quick call to his dad letting him know what was going on. Dad was relieved to hear Drew was okay but appalled at the turn of events.

After hanging up with his father, Drew knocked on the connecting door to Sami's room. They were scheduled to fly to Victoria, BC, in a few hours.

The door between their rooms opened. Sami was

dressed in one of the outfits purchased for her to replace her wardrobe, which had gone up in flames. The deep blue of her jeans and blouse made the blue in her eyes pop. Her blond hair was clipped back on the sides with barrettes, making her look younger than her twenty-eight years as he'd seen she was when he checked her ID. She greeted him with a smile. "Good morning. I hope you got some rest."

"A little. How about you?"

She shrugged. "I slept some."

Eyeing the bandage on her head, he asked, "Did you change the dressing on your wound?"

She nodded. "You?"

He held out a clean bandage. "Would you change it for me? It's out of my reach."

"Of course." She swiftly and efficiently removed the old bandage for a new one. Her cool touch burned through him, making his senses hyperaware of her. He caught a whiff of apple shampoo. It must have been on her list.

She was just like the shampoo. Tart and sweet.

When she finished, he turned around to thank her, but the words lodged in his throat as his gaze landed on her mouth. Would she taste tart or sweet or both?

Her lips parted slightly. The temperature in the room seemed to hike up a few degrees. His gaze met hers. She stared at him, her eyes wide and questioning.

He stepped back. "We should go."

One side of her mouth tipped upward and determination flooded her expression. She held up a small knapsack in one hand and gestured to a carry-on suitcase. She'd bought both yesterday at the shop next to the hotel. Since she carried her wallet in her pants pocket, she still had her ID, cash and credit cards. She'd also bought him an identical traveler case, which he'd filled with the things Agent Foster had procured. "I'm all packed. Not that I had much to put in here."

They checked out of the hotel and were driven by two FBI agents to her bank so she could retrieve the copies of her research from her safe-deposit box. Then they were taken to Portland International Airport. Once there they headed straight to the security office and went through the necessary process to board the plane bound for Canada.

Sami was convinced there was another victim somewhere in the city of Victoria. Drew hoped she was wrong, yet he had a feeling she was right. The senseless killings grated on his conscience. Birdman had to be stopped. But how many more people would die before that happened?

On the plane, he tucked his and Sami's carry-on cases in the overhead bin. Then he slid into the seat next to Sami. She'd placed the knapsack containing all the information she had on Birdman at her feet. He didn't blame her for not wanting to let the contents out of her sight.

She had purchased a map of Victoria at one of the gift shops in the airport. Now she had it spread out on her lap and her new smartphone in one hand and a red pen in the other. "I'm marking all the hotels I can find using the internet."

"That's a very productive idea." She was a marvel, this FBI agent. He suspected she'd go far within her agency.

After a short layover in Seattle, they landed in Victoria with a map full of red dots.

"Let's head to The Grand Hotel first," Sami said. "I want to double-check there's nothing there."

Drew didn't blame her. She'd been on the trail of this killer for six months. She knew how devious he was. Birdman could have anticipated they'd send the local authorities to check out the hotel and waited until after they'd completed their search to stage his victim in a room for Sami to find.

They rented a car. They both wanted to drive, which didn't surprise Drew. He'd already assessed her need for control. It was easy to identify because on many levels he, too, had control issues. They flipped a coin. Heads—he won.

"You drove last time." She reached for the coin on the pavement. "Let's go two out of three."

He laughed and opened the passenger door for her. "You drive on the way back."

"Whatever," she muttered, slipping the coin into her jeans pocket before climbing in.

He slid behind the wheel. Soon they exited the airport area. He took Highway 17, which would take them all the way into Victoria, the capital city of British Columbia. The scenic views of the many different landscapes that made up the island, from mountain ranges to rugged coastline, held Sami enthralled.

He had to admit he thought his country the most beautiful. Especially in the Pacific Northwest. He'd visited Vancouver Island as a kid on holiday with his parents before his mom had taken off, leaving him and his dad to fend for themselves. Those were some of his fondest memories, as well as the most pain filled. He'd also come here with Gretchen on their first anniversary. Shaking his head, he pushed the memories aside.

The city sat on the southern tip of Vancouver Island and had a large port area, which allowed the town to fill with tourists disembarking from cruise ships, as well as those venturing over the water on the ferry from the United States and Canada's mainland. A mix of old-world England and modern Canada, the city was both quaint and progressive.

Drew maneuvered the rental sedan through mid-morning downtown traffic and found a spot in front of The Grand Hotel. After obtaining a ticket from the parking meter machine, Drew and Sami approached the hotel entrance.

As they'd been told, the hotel was under construction. Huge sheets of plastic draped down the sides and scaffolding zigzagged across the exterior. They entered the lobby and went directly to the reception desk to ask for the manager.

The hotel definitely needed an update. The tired and worn carpeting and the faux-leather furniture circa 1970 made Drew feel as though he'd stepped back in time.

A tall well-dressed man approached. His graying hair was slicked back from his face and emphasized his large nose and square jaw. "I'm Maurice Stranvic, the manager. How can I be of assistance?"

Drew showed the man his badge. "I'm Inspector Kelley, RCMP, and this is Special Agent Bennett with the FBI. We have reason to believe a crime has been committed on the premises."

Maurice frowned. "The police were here yesterday. They searched the building and didn't find anything amiss. As you can see we are undergoing some renovations. We've been closed for the past five days. No one but employees and construction workers have been on-site."

"We'd like to conduct our own search," Drew replied, his gaze intent on the man. Was there something he was trying to hide?

"What is it you are hoping to find?" Maurice asked, his voice rising slightly.

"Sorry, sir. We can't discuss an ongoing investigation," Sami said, her voice courteous and even-toned. "Though we would appreciate it if you could check your hotel register and see if a James Clark or a Melinda Watson ever stayed here?"

Drew had to give Sami credit for her professionalism. And he hadn't thought to inquire about the woman— the victim they'd discovered in Vancouver.

"Why is an American FBI agent investigating on Canadian soil?" Maurice questioned.

"A joint effort," Drew said in a tone that effectively closed the subject. "May we proceed?"

"Of course." Maurice led them to the reception desk. He opened a laptop and typed. After a few moments, he shook his head. "I did a search on those two names. Neither one has stayed in our establishment."

Drew wasn't sure if he was more disappointed or afraid. Would they find another clue that would lead them to another location and another body or be left with a dead end?

Maurice beckoned over a young Asian man who looked to be barely out of his teens.

"Sir, what can I do for you?" the man asked.

The hotel manager gestured to Drew and Sami. "Take Inspector Kelley and FBI Agent Bennett on a tour of the building. Leave nothing unchecked." Maurice turned back to them. "Liam will show you around. If you'll excuse me."

Drew watched the man saunter back behind the reception desk, then turned to greet their guide. "Hello, Liam. Do you know the hotel well?"

Liam nodded. "Very well indeed, sir. My mother and my grandmother both worked here when I was a boy. I know every nook and cranny of this place."

"Good—then you won't skip over anything," Sami said. "We need to peek into every room."

Checking each room on all three floors ate up the afternoon. And they found nothing. No bodies, no blood, no birds.

"Liam, has there been much crime in the hotel?" Sami asked, pointing to the small camera bolted to the ceiling near the staircase.

"Not in recent years. Not since the hotel beefed up their security system. Before that we'd have the occasional loafer or thief try to sneak into rooms," Liam replied as he descended the staircase.

Drew and Sami followed close on his heels.

"Though, now that I think of it, thirty years ago there was a murder here. Some lady was strangled and..." He paused for dramatic effect. "And mutilated."

Sami stopped in the middle of the stairs. "What?"

Drew understood her shock; he felt the same stunned sensation.

Liam paused to glance back. "It's not something the management talks about, but my grandmother was working here at the time. She said the woman and her child had been staying in the hotel on vacation when it happened."

Drew exchanged a pointed look with Sami. They needed to find out more about the murder.

They thanked Liam and Maurice, then headed out of the hotel. The temperature had dropped while the sun went down over the horizon.

"I don't think it's a coincidence that Birdman left the hotel matchbook," Sami said while they walked toward the parking garage. "But what does a thirty-year-old murder have to do with Birdman's killing spree?"

"Only way to find out is to pull the case file."

With a wry twist of her lips, Sami said, "Let's hope the Victoria police have had their records digitized or we might be in for a long night."

As it turned out, VicPD's digitized records went back only twenty years. Budget cuts and reallocation of funds had kept the information division of the police department from continuing with the uploading of files.

True to Sami's prediction, the night stretched and so did her nerves. She and Drew were escorted to a storage facility beneath the courthouse where boxes of files going as far back as the 1800s were stacked in rows, one box atop another. Layers of dust coated everything.

It took several hours before they found the correct box corresponding to the year that Liam had said the murder at The Grand Hotel had taken place.

Now Sami stared at the cold case file laid out on a table for the murder of an American woman named Becca Kraft, age thirty-five, a waitress and the single mother of one.

"The method of strangulation and mutilation are eerily similar to the cases you have attributed to Birdman," Drew said.

She couldn't quell the shudder that rippled through her as she snapped a photo with her phone of each page of the file. "But the question is, are we dealing with the same killer?"

"This could have been his first kill," Drew stated grimly.

"If so, then why tip us off?" She snorted and answered her own question. "He's a serial killer and apparently in desperate need of recognition."

"Or we're dealing with a copycat and he wants us to know who he's copying."

"But according to the investigator's notes the details of Becca's murder were never made public," Sami pointed out. "Whoever killed Becca Kraft is either still killing or revealed his method to someone else."

"An apprentice," Drew said, his tone making it clear how distasteful he found the idea.

"Possibly." Sami finished with the photos and replaced the file in the box. "If we're dealing with the same killer—let's say he committed this crime when he was an adult, like twenty-one—he'd be at least fifty-one now. That gives us an idea of our perp's age."

"Now that we know the victim in Vancouver wasn't the first time Birdman crossed the boundary between our countries, I want to head back to the VicPD and use their database."

"That's a good idea. And I can have Agent Granger search the US databases going back to the mid-'80s." She hated to think of all the victims that could have suffered at Birdman's hands over the years.

They returned to the Victoria Police Department headquarters, passing the colorful five-foot-tall totem pole gracing the front entrance to the building. Sami stared at the birdlike feature at the top. It struck her as ironic to see a bird carving. "Do you know what kind of bird that is?"

Drew studied the carving. "Looks like a thunderbird. He is a symbol of power, protection and strength."

"It looks nothing like the silly bird drawings," Sami remarked, her voice echoing with the frustration tying her insides into knots.

This beautiful carving stood for something unique and wonderful, while Birdman's drawings brought death and destruction.

Inside the police station, Drew met with the chief of police and was granted access to the Canadian Police Information Centre database. Sami put a call in to her boss, who promised to phone if he found anything useful in the US database.

Sami joined Drew as he trolled through the various case files on the CPIC, looking for similar unsolved murders.

By the time they were done, they had ten cold cases that matched their criteria, all within the past two years.

"We need a place to regroup," Drew said. "I have a friend who owns a cottage near the shore. I'll see if it's available."

"That sounds good but we still have to check all the hotels," Sami reminded him. "Just in case." Not continuing the search for Birdman's latest victim wasn't an option.

"You're right. Let me talk to the chief. We'll need help."

She held up her phone. "Could we make printed copies of the pictures I took of Becca Kraft's file?"

Palming her phone, he said, "I'll see what I can do." He walked away in search of the VicPD's head officer.

While she waited, she moved to the lobby, where she'd spotted a drink vending machine. Only she didn't have any Canadian coins.

A man stepped up next to her. "Too many choices?"

Naturally cautious, she stepped away, giving herself room if she needed to defend herself. She looked at the man. His red hair seemed too bright to be natural and he had a ring in his nose. His overall appearance reminded her of the days of grunge bands. It was hard to tell his age. The guy could have been in his thirties. Maybe younger, maybe older. "I want a bottle of water," she explained, "but I only have American coins."

The man smiled. One of his incisors had a gold cap. "Here, let me."

"Oh, you don't have to do that," she said, but he was already moving. He stuck a few coins in, pressed the button for the water. When the bottle thumped into the bin, he reached down to retrieve it.

Handing the bottle to her, he said, "Enjoy."

"Thank you." She took the water and the man strode out the front lobby doors and disappeared into the now dark night.

She twisted off the cap and took a swig of the water. As the bottle tilted upward, her gaze snagged on something attached to the label. Frowning, she straightened the bottle and turned it so she could see the other side.

A tiny yellow sticker with a small bird stared back at her.

Her breath stalled. Her heart froze. Birdman.

A shot of adrenaline galvanized her into action. She

raced out of the building, searching for the red-haired grunge-garbed man. He was nowhere in sight.

She began to shake as she backed toward the police station doors.

Behind her she heard the swoosh of the doors opening and she whirled around, her hand reaching for her weapon.

"Sami?" Drew held up his hands palms out. "What's wrong?"

Relaxing her stance but not her senses, she once again scanned the street, the sidewalks, the buildings all around. Where had Birdman disappeared to?

"He was here." She held out the bottle, using her index finger and thumb in the hope of preserving any fingerprints he might have left behind, but if he'd stayed true to form, there wouldn't be any. She didn't remember seeing gloves. "He touched this."

Drew frowned. "Who was here?"

"Birdman." She swallowed back the realization that crashed through her at full throttle. "Birdman followed us here."

EIGHT

"Why would he toy with me like this?" Sami asked, but she knew Drew didn't have the answer. No one but Birdman knew why he did anything. And that truth festered deep inside her like a sore.

After reviewing the station's security videos, Sami and Drew were now sequestered in the chief of police's office. Drew remained standing at her side while she sat in a chair facing Chief Heyes, who took his seat behind a wide desk.

The Canadian flag hung from a pole in the corner. Framed certificates and brass-plated plaques hung on the walls. A filing cabinet behind the chief sported a plethora of photos, some of people Sami guessed to be his family and friends, others of officers mugging for the camera.

Sami wiped her palms on her thighs. She despised the sense of powerlessness seeping into her marrow.

The video from the camera in the lobby showed the red-haired man had entered the station shortly after Sami and Drew had arrived. He must have followed them from The Grand Hotel. Had he been waiting there for her? He seemed to constantly be one step ahead of her.

The man kept his face turned from the camera as he approached the desk, spoke to the sergeant, then headed down the hall for the restroom. He returned to the lobby a minute after Sami, as if he'd been in the shadows waiting for her to appear. To what end?

First he taunted her with his bird drawings and bread crumbs, leading her on a wild chase from crime scene to crime scene. Then he blew up her house and tried to run her down, and then he showed up here, acting like a Good Samaritan.

"That was bold, coming into the police station like that," Drew stated.

Her skin crawled. Birdman had been so close. If she'd only realized… Her fingers curled into fists.

"I'll interview Sergeant Dodge myself," Chief Heyes said, referring to the desk sergeant who'd talked to Birdman. Drew had explained to the chief the theory that a serial killer was on the loose in both the United States and Canada. "Agent Bennett, can you recall the man's eye color?"

The chief was an imposing man in his sixties with a head of white hair and sharp green eyes that were fixed on her.

"Dark. He was at least six foot. Caucasian. The red hair wasn't natural. Too bright, clownish, even. Possibly a wig, if not, definitely a bad dye job." She closed her eyes and conjured up his image. Her lids popped open. Something about his face bothered her. "He had makeup on. Like theatrical pancake base." She'd used the stuff during plays in high school. "And a nose ring."

"We'll disseminate his description to the rank and file," Chief Heyes assured them as he made notes on his computer. "Do you have a safe place to go? I could have you set up in a safe house within the hour."

"I've got us covered," Drew said. "We'll be going to a friend's. The place is about forty minutes from here."

"I'll send one of our uniformed officers with you," the chief said.

Sami was thankful for the extra backup. "What about the hotels? We know Birdman's here, so there's a body out there somewhere needing to be found."

"We'll take care of the search, Agent Bennett," Heyes said. "Thank you for your help."

Her hand tightened around the map on which she'd marked all the hotels in and around Victoria. She wanted to be a part of the search. It was her job to find the victims, her job to bring them justice. She drummed the fingers of her free hand on her knee.

Drew put his hand on her shoulder. "It's better if we aren't involved in this search. It may be exactly what Birdman expects."

She stilled, disconcerted by how easily Drew read her. She blew out a breath of frustration.

"You're right." She turned to the chief. "Do you have a full-size map of North America?"

"I'm sure we can rummage one up for you." He rose. "I'll handpick the officer to accompany you."

"We appreciate that," Drew said.

When the chief left the office, Sami stood and paced. "Birdman must have followed us from Portland. I don't recall seeing him on the flight. A guy like that stands out."

"We'll catch him."

His quiet reassurance halted her steps. "You sound so sure." She wanted to believe him. To believe *in* him. "I've been three steps behind him for the past six months."

He closed the distance between them and pulled her into his embrace. "But you were on your own before. Now you have a partner. In fact, you have a whole team on both sides of the border."

She tilted her head back to look at him. The word *partner* echoed through her mind. After Ian's injuries, she hadn't had a specific partner for longer than a single assignment. A team, however, sounded good. No one getting too attached to each other. "I pray a team will be enough."

"It will be." His hand smoothed down her back, leaving a trail of fire in its wake. "You have to have faith that good will triumph over evil."

Knowing she should step out of his arms but unable to bring herself to do so, she laid her cheek against his heart. "I try to, but sometimes the injustice gets to me."

Her faith wobbled at times. Like when she'd learned of Lisa's death. And with each victim she'd found.

She wanted to trust God, to rely on Him as she'd been taught to do growing up. Some days her faith was the only thing keeping her going. Other days she questioned God, questioned her faith. "I don't understand why God allows so much evil to exist. He's all-powerful, so why doesn't He wipe out the evil?"

"He could, but then who would be left? I'm certainly not without sin. And if all sin is evil, then…"

She couldn't refute his logic, but that didn't alleviate her frustration and anger at the senselessness of it all. She stepped out of his arms and stared at the smiling faces of the chief's family pinned to the side of the metal filing cabinet. "Yeah, I hear what you're saying.

And you're right. I get it. 'He without sin cast the first stone' and all that. But it doesn't make injustice any easier to accept."

With the crook of his finger, he drew her gaze back to him. "No, it doesn't. We do what we can and leave the rest to God."

With grim determination, she nodded. "And what we can do is figure out Birdman's pattern and then flush him out like bird dogs."

Drew grinned. "There you go. We're big dogs with big teeth. He doesn't stand a chance."

She smiled back; she couldn't help herself. His sense of humor appealed to her. He didn't take himself too seriously, whereas she took herself way too seriously. A fact she accepted about herself, especially after the fiasco with Ian.

They had been partnered for a year before their relationship took a turn toward romance. Then things changed. He'd no longer treated her as his partner in the field.

Instead he'd constantly felt the need to protect her rather than having her back and allowing her to have his. His inability to separate their personal relationship from their professional one had cost him the use of one leg and ended his career as a field agent.

Chief Heyes returned to the office and handed Sami the map she'd requested. "Here you go. Can I ask what this is for?"

Sami looked to Drew to explain since this was his country and he'd done the research.

"Using the CPIC, we've matched a number of unsolved murders with similarities to the ones that Agent Bennett has compiled. We believe this Birdman is operating on both sides of the border. We hope by study-ing the case files and locations we can come up with something that will help catch him."

Heyes nodded with apparent approval. "All right. Let me know what my department can do to help you." He turned and waved in a tall blond-haired brown-eyed uniformed officer. "This is Chet Brown. He'll accom-pany you to your friend's house."

After the introductions, Drew asked, "Chet, do you have a personal car and street clothes?"

"Yes, sir," Chet replied.

Sami shot Drew a questioning look.

"If Birdman followed us, then he knows what our rental car looks like. I don't want a repeat of Portland."

"Right." That had been a close one. "Good thinking."

"I'll go change," Chet said. "My truck is parked in the lot out back." He hustled away.

Sami turned to Drew. "We need to stop at a store on the way out of town. We'll need more bandages and toothbrushes since our stuff is in the rental."

"I could send an officer to retrieve your things from the car," Heyes offered.

Drew shook his head. "The best thing will be to not have anyone approach the car. If Birdman is sitting on it as I suspect, we don't want him knowing we're not coming back to the car."

"All right, then. And in case you're right, I'll have officers keep a watch on it for the suspect. Let's keep each other apprised of any developments," Heyes said.

"Yes, sir." Drew shook Heyes's hand. "Thank you for your cooperation."

"Always," Heyes said. To Sami he said, "Thank you

for all your work, Agent Bennett. I thank you on behalf of my country and my city."

Agitation battered her as Sami shook his hand and hoped that her work would be enough to capture Birdman before he could do any more harm.

Drew peered through the front window of Chet's truck looking for the house number of his friend's cottage. The drive from Victoria was on a winding road that took them through dense forest broken by the occasional residence. Though Drew knew Chet was alert to any sign of being followed, Drew had kept an eye on the side mirror, as well.

The three of them were squished in the cab of Chet's large pickup. Drew sat next to the passenger door, Sami in the middle with Chet driving. He leaned into her to keep his back from bumping the leather seat. She was soft in all the right places, yet he knew a core of strength lay within her.

After leaving the police station they'd stopped outside the city limits at a Thrifty Foods to buy toiletries, over-the-counter pain medicine and food since neither of them had eaten since breakfast.

The injury to Drew's back protested the day's activities, and the bouncing of the truck didn't help. He would have to take one of the strong painkillers tonight if he hoped to get any sleep.

"That's it there," Drew said as the truck's headlights shone on the mailbox, revealing the correct number. The place was dark inside. The light of the high moon cast shadows on the exterior.

Chet pulled the truck into the driveway and shut off the engine.

"Who owns this place?" Sami asked when they were out of the truck and at the front door.

Drew hunted for the house key beneath a potted plant to the left of the door. "An old college buddy. I called him earlier to see if the cottage was free."

He found the key and slid it into the lock. The door opened soundlessly. Drew entered with his hand on his holstered gun, found a table lamp and switched it on. In the living room, the hardwood floors were covered with geometric-patterned rugs. A plush-looking chesterfield sat against one wall and faced floor-to-ceiling patio doors that provided a view of the Salish Sea inlet. Moonlight danced on the water and illuminated a long dock.

Sami walked to the gray stone fireplace, which was a focal point for the room. "Nice place." She ran her hand over the stone. "I like this. Very cool."

"There are three bedrooms. Two on the main floor and a small one in the loft space. One washroom, down the hall past the kitchen," Drew said.

Sami nodded and moved to the small dining table. She spread the map Chief Heyes had given her over the top. "Let's get to work."

With wry amusement, Drew said, "How about you start on that and I'll fix us something to eat?"

"I can take care of the food after I do a perimeter check," Chet offered.

Drew appreciated the younger man's help. "Skookum."

Chet saluted and headed out the door.

Sami cocked her head. "What's 'skookum'?"

"Means great or excellent."

She laughed. "Good to know." She sobered. "Do you have a pen I can use?"

"I'm sure there's one around here somewhere." Drew moved into the kitchen to search the drawers. He found a box of pencil crayons and carried them to her. "No pens but I found pencil crayons."

She took the box from him, their fingers brushing against each other and creating a warm glow that spread over him. "These will work. And by the by, in the States we call them colored pencils. Crayons are made from colored wax."

"Embrace our differences, eh?" He grinned at her.

"Sure, eh?" she shot back.

She took out two pencils and handed him a green one, while she took a blue one. "I'll work on the US side, marking all the places Birdman has hit along with the date. If you do the same on your side of the map, maybe we can figure out if there is some rhyme or reason to his madness."

"Ah, a little Shakespeare. 'Was there ever any man thus beaten out of season, When in the why and the wherefore is neither rhyme nor reason?'"

Sami looked at him through her lashes, momentarily pausing her task. "Okay. If you say so."

Chet returned with an all clear and went into the kitchen. The sounds of pots clanking and cupboards opening and shutting provided background noise as they worked.

"Not a fan of the Bard?" Drew checked his list and began circling cities and writing the dates of the corresponding crimes on the map.

"Can't say that I am."

"No Romeo or Juliet for you, eh? I thought most women liked that one at least. It's a love story."

She arched an eyebrow. "It's a tragedy. I don't do tragedies."

"You see enough in your work." He understood the sentiment. Anyone in law enforcement tended to see the world through jaded eyes. "But you believe in love, right?"

"Oh, you want to go there, do you?" She shook her head. "I'm not sure we've known each other long enough to have that conversation."

He glanced up, surprised by her prevarication.

Interesting. Had she not fared well in the love department? Not that he had any room to talk.

Curious, he said, "We may not have known each other for very long but I feel like in the short time we've worked together we've already gone through more than most partners."

She paused, her hand hovering over the map. Her gaze lifted. "We're partners, working together on a case. There's no need for this to get personal." With that she went back to work.

He watched her for a moment, not sure how he felt about the boundary she'd just laid down. He was usually the one to limit involvement when it came to women. But that was dating, not work related.

He'd never had a female partner. Not that he would have been opposed. Though the RCMP employed women, the percentage of females was only a quarter of the sum total of officers.

"You mentioned you had a partner once," Drew said. "What happened to him?"

Sami straightened and met his gaze. Her eyes flashed

with pain and anger. "He took a bullet meant for me. It left him lame in one leg."

Ah. She carried guilt for his injury like a weight around her neck. "And that makes you angry."

"Yes. Ian broke from his defensive position because he was worried about me instead of focusing on the job. If he'd stayed put, he would have stopped the suspect before he got a shot off."

"You two were involved outside of the job?" He saw that his guess hit its mark by the way red crept up her neck and stained her cheeks.

"A mistake I will not repeat."

"You have nothing to worry about here. Romance is the last thing I'm looking for. Been down that terrifying road once already."

It was her turn to quiz him. She arched an eyebrow. "Bad breakup?"

"Divorced. I married my college sweetheart. The marriage lasted two years before she decided to upgrade to a doctor."

Sympathy tinged her expression. "Ouch."

He shrugged, hoping for nonchalance. The scar on his heart still stung. "Yeah, well, it was a lesson learned. Love doesn't last."

She frowned. "I don't believe that. My parents and my grandparents have all had long marriages. And they'd all say it takes work."

"So you are a closet romantic." He wasn't sure why that pleased him. "Just not when it comes to the workplace."

She appeared startled by his observation. "Yes, I'd say that's true. But I still don't like how *Romeo and Juliet* ends."

He chuckled. "Noted. What happened between you and Ian after he was shot?"

"We broke up. He moved to Washington, DC, and decided to go to law school."

"You didn't go with him." If she had, Drew might never have met her. That thought didn't sit well. "Why not?"

"I wasn't in love with him. At least not enough to uproot my life to follow him."

He liked her honesty. There was no pretense. She was who she was and made no excuses for it. She was the kind of woman a man hoped to find. The kind of woman he'd hoped to find. But unfortunately, their lives would never intersect after this case.

Once their partnership successfully brought down Birdman—and Drew was confident they would—he and Sami would go their separate ways. He would return to Vancouver and she would return to Portland. He pushed aside the hollow feeling invading him at the prospect of not seeing Sami after this.

As the scent of spicy meat filled the house, Drew concentrated on finishing his list. When he did, he stepped back.

The Canadian side of the map had twelve circles, including the victim in Vancouver and Becca Kraft's murder in Victoria, spanning the width of the country. His heart sped up.

Sami finished, as well. "Do you have any tape?"

He'd seen some in the drawer in the kitchen. He collected the clear tape dispenser and returned to the dining area. Sami held the map flat against the wall. He taped the four corners to the wall. They both stepped back to view the map as a whole. Twenty-two circles. Twelve on the Canadian side and ten on the US side.

Drew swallowed back the bile that suddenly turned his stomach and chased away his appetite.

Sami picked up a red pencil crayon and connected the string of murders by their dates. A clear ping-ponging pattern marching across both countries emerged.

"Do you see it?" Sami whispered.

"Unfortunately, I do."

Birdman's macabre killing spree alternated between cities in both Canada and the United States. And the frequency of the murders had steadily increased.

NINE

After dinner Sami and Drew resumed their examination of the map. Sami had barely eaten Chet's meal. Though the chicken and broccoli dish was excellent, her appetite had deserted her. The beach bungalow grew colder. She'd snatched a colorful afghan from the couch and wrapped it around her shoulders.

"If Birdman's first murder happened here in Victoria thirty years ago and the next one here—" Sami pointed to the map where a circle surrounded the city of Detroit "—that's a twenty-eight-year span between the Victoria murder and the Detroit murder."

She turned to Drew, wanting, needing some clarity. His hair was mussed from running his fingers through the thick dark strands. Her own fingers itched to smooth the longer pieces of hair off his forehead. She pulled the blanket tighter around her as if that could somehow contain her fascination with Drew.

He stared at the map with a grim and horrified expression that mirrored her own feelings. The grisly killings spanned two countries and twenty-two different cities. With the time between murders rapidly growing closer together.

The acceleration corresponded to when Sami began to connect the crimes during the course of her investigation into her best friend's murder. The simmering anger that was never far from the surface heated her flesh. She shrugged off the afghan.

"What happened two years ago that set him off again?" Drew said. "And where has he been for twenty-eight years?"

"Maybe he's been in prison. We'll need to check our respective databases for similar murders to Becca Kraft's for the same time period."

"Agreed. If he was released two years ago, that would explain the long time span."

Frustration pounded at her temple. "But it doesn't explain why these victims? Why these cities?"

"And how is he crossing the border so frequently without being flagged? Our two countries share information for border control purposes." He picked up his mug of coffee but didn't drink. "If someone came and went this frequently, an agent would be curious as to why, especially if the person has a criminal record."

She appreciated his sharp mind. "Unless Birdman's job permits him to move back and forth without much questioning."

They'd had this thought before. Seeing just how much their suspect traveled between their two countries alerted them to the need to revisit the discussion.

Sami grabbed a blank piece of paper from the notebook they'd brought from the police station. "A commercial vehicle could easily move back and forth with little hassle as long as the paperwork was legit. However, the time issue is problematic." She wrote down "truck driver."

"A convicted felon would be flagged at the border crossing. Unless he's going by an alias," Drew pointed out. "We also need to consider train employees, bus employees and airline employees."

Sami wrote those options down. She liked the give-and-take of working with him. "We've ruled out an airport baggage handler because that would require more than one suspect. I still maintain Birdman is acting alone."

"I agree. No baggage handler."

It would take a great deal of time and manpower to check every employee who had a legitimate reason for repeatedly crossing the border. She studied the map some more. "We can try to narrow down the type of profession we're looking for by excluding cities that don't have airports, train depots or bus service."

"We'll need a computer to look up the various services and their routes," Drew said. "Major airports are easier to pinpoint, but there are regional and municipal airports, as well."

"I brought my computer," Chet said from the doorway of the dining room. He'd insisted on doing the cleanup after dinner so they could get back to work.

Drew and Sami gave him the quick rundown on Birdman and his killing spree.

"It's kind of like finding the proverbial needle in a haystack, or in this case one murderer among a billion people," Chet commented before going outside to get his computer from his truck.

Sami set down her pencil and picked up her phone to view the pictures she'd taken of Becca Kraft's file. "Why did Birdman point me to Becca Kraft's murder? And where does James Clark fit in?"

"Our mystery man," Drew said. "Victim or perp?"

"Your intel pegged Clark as a family man and business owner. Most serial killers appear to be normal people living normal lives. So why not him?" She shuddered with revulsion. "We need more information about James Clark."

"Agreed. The IBETs team's working to find him."

Chet returned and set up his computer at the dining table. "Oops, forgot the power cord. Be right back." He headed outside once again.

Something nagged at the back of Sami's mind. She read the case notes again. "Becca Kraft, age thirty-five was found strangled, her body mutilated postmortem in her hotel room. No particulates to identify the attacker. The medical examiner confirmed cause of death as asphyxiation."

"The same as the others," Drew said.

"Only in Becca's case, there were signs of sexual activity prior to death. That doesn't fit with Birdman's MO." She yanked the clip out of her hair and shook her head. It felt good to have her hair unbound.

"No, it doesn't."

She slanted him a glance. He stared at her hair. Self-conscious, she reached up to smooth it. "What?"

"I didn't realize your hair was so long."

The appreciation in his voice made her blink. An odd flutter began in her tummy. She dropped her eyes to the report in front of her. Forcing herself to focus, she said, "Becca and her son were on vacation according to the police report."

"Where was the kid at the time of the murder?"

She scanned the photocopies of the report and studied the handwritten notations. "According to the detective on the case, the boy was hiding in the closet when the police arrived. He was too traumatized to tell them anything."

Drew moved closer to look over her shoulder. His breath tickled her hair. "Does the report give the kid's name?"

"No." She turned her head to look at him. His face was so close. His mouth just inches from hers. Her heart skipped a beat. The craving to kiss him almost overwhelmed her. With more willpower than she'd thought herself capable of, she glanced back at the papers, grateful for her hair, which fell forward, creating a barrier that separated him from her line of sight. "He's only referred to as the Kraft boy."

Why was her voice so breathless? *Get a grip!*

It took effort to concentrate on the report. "Oh, here's something—Becca had a sister, name Lonnie Freeman, who took custody of the child."

"Maybe Lonnie could shed some light on why her sister was murdered."

"I'm sure if she could have, she would have years ago."

Her hand stilled on the report as she felt Drew lift a strand of her hair and rub it between his fingers. She couldn't help looking up to watch his fingers slide over the ends of her hair.

He met her gaze. "I like your hair down."

Not sure what to do with that bit of information, she nodded.

After a charged moment in which neither seemed able to look away, he let her hair fall back to her shoulder.

Chet came back through the door. "Got it." He held up the power cord.

Drew moved away from Sami and cleared his throat before he began to speak, but his voice was still thick. "The boy could have told her something that she might not have realized was significant. It could be worth talking to her."

Sami, too, had to give her head a mental shake. Transferring her attention from the potent man at her side was not easy. She sat up straighter and forced her focus back on the case. "I'll call my agency's tech guru in Portland. Jordon will track Lonnie down."

"While you do that I'll check in and see if there's news on James Clark." Drew took his phone and moved into the living room.

Sami called Jordon, the Portland FBI's technology whiz. She gave him all the information she had and within minutes Jordon had Lonnie's contact info. Lonnie Freeman lived and worked in Seattle, Washington.

Drew returned to the dining room giving his report. "Still no sign of James Clark. His employees filed a missing-person report."

"Not the wife?"

"Apparently not. Any luck tracking down Becca Kraft's sister?"

"Yep, she's a nurse at Virginia Mason Hospital in Seattle."

"Tomorrow we'll take the ferry over. It will be more expedient."

"I've never been on a ferry," Sami admitted.

"This time of year the water should be smooth," Drew said. "We can stand on the deck and might even see orcas swimming in the sound. The season usually runs from April to September."

"Cool." She took the map off the wall and rolled it

up, then put a piece of tape along the edge to keep it from unrolling. "I've always wanted to see a whale up close. Though I never expected it would happen while chasing down a serial killer."

The thought of sharing the experience with him brought a heated flush to her skin. An image formed in her mind. Them together standing at the railing of a ship with a vast body of water stretching before them, his arms around her, buffeting her from the wind. Only in her version they weren't tracking a killer. They were just two people enjoying life together.

Reining in her runaway imagination, she forced herself to face reality because that scenario wasn't going to happen.

The next morning, Chet drove Sami and Drew to the ferry service in Victoria that would take them across the Strait of Juan de Fuca into the Puget Sound to dock in Seattle. Sami eyed the huge ship bobbing at the harbor and bit her lip. She hoped she didn't get seasick. This would be her first time on a boat this big. A kayak wasn't comparable.

At the customs gate, they showed their IDs and filled out the proper forms to board the *Victoria Clipper*, a large vessel capable of carrying over three hundred passengers.

Sami and Drew made their way to the upper observation deck. Though the sun shone bright, the breeze coming off the Pacific Ocean was cool.

Drew stood beside her. In his requisite white button-down shirt, he still looked like a banker, but she knew he was so much more than he appeared. *Gallant*, that was a word she would use to describe him. And he had the wound to prove it. Self-consciously, she touched the bandage on her head. Her own injury was healing nicely.

Soon the roar of the ferry engine drowned out the cry of the seagulls flying overhead and the large vessel pulled away from the dock. Within minutes the ferry picked up speed, cutting through the water at a rapid clip. The wind whipped Sami's hair into tangles. She gathered the mass in one hand and held on.

"Do you want to go inside?"

She had to read his lips to understand what he was saying. For a moment his mouth distracted her. She liked the shape of his lips, the strength of character in his jaw. The way he was so calm and steady. He was a good man. Solid and dependable. Honorable.

He arched an eyebrow, making her realize she hadn't answered his question. Appreciating his thoughtfulness, she shook her head and yelled to be heard over the wind and the engine, "Not yet."

The view as they left Vancouver Island behind was spectacular. Against the backdrop of the mountains, Victoria, with its unique and beautiful architecture, grew smaller as the boat sped farther away. Spray from the boat's wake sprinkled her face with salty ocean water.

She would've liked to enjoy the scenery more but the rocking movement of the boat sent her stomach rolling.

Afraid she'd be sick all over the deck, she pointed to the stairwell leading down to the enclosed seating area. Drew followed as she headed down the stairs. They found two empty seats on the right side of the vessel near the large rectangular window. She flopped into her seat. Unfortunately, sitting made her nausea worse.

"You're turning green," Drew said, concern in his voice. "You should have said you get seasick. We could have flown again."

A plane sounded like a good idea now but for expediency's sake she'd thought the ferry a better option. Not so much now.

"I didn't know I would get seasick," she shot back. "First time on a ferry, remember?"

"Put your head between your knees," Drew instructed.

She did as he suggested. He rubbed little circles on her back. A nice distraction that helped—for about two seconds. She popped upright and clamped a hand over her mouth. "I'm going to be sick."

Drew stood and pointed to the restroom. "There. Hurry."

She scooted past him, waving him off when he moved to follow. The last thing she needed was him witnessing her humiliating herself. She hustled toward the restrooms, but of course there was a line.

"Excuse me, going to be sick," she said, though her hand muffled her voice and she wasn't sure anyone heard her.

When no one moved out of her way, she abandoned the line and headed for the staircase leading to the front of the boat. A shadowy figure blocked the exit.

Sami ran up the steps. "Move!"

As the person stepped aside, she barreled forward, barely making it to the railing before she dry-heaved over the side of the boat. Apparently, her stomach wasn't willing to give up her breakfast so easily.

Once the worst of the nausea subsided, she took several cleansing breaths, filling her lungs with fresh air. Just as she was beginning to calm down, she was grabbed from behind and lifted off her feet, then tilted over the railing toward the churning water below.

Panic roared through her and echoed in her scream. The fight for survival kicked in. She clung to the railing to keep from going overboard, the metal tubing digging deep into her torso. She twisted to defend herself as her assailant continued to force her over the side of the boat.

She teetered on the railing. She let go with one hand to grasp the assailant's jacket, her mind screaming with recognition.

"You!" It was the same red-haired man from the Victoria police station. Only now his eyes were a cold light blue. Shivers of fear cascaded over her flesh.

"Hey!"

Drew's shout reached through the fear clouding Sami's brain. Her heart surged in her chest and a sense of relief gave her a boost of energy. Drew wouldn't let this man throw her overboard. She rocked forward, away from the edge, as the man released his hold. Her feet hit the deck with a jarring thud.

Her assailant scurried to the other side of the deck and flung himself over the edge. Sami's mouth dropped open. Her mind struggled to grasp what she'd just seen.

"Are you okay?" Drew gripped her by the elbow.

"It's him!" she shouted, and tugged him to where the guy had disappeared. She peered over the side of the boat, expecting to see the man in the water. Instead the red-haired man clung to the piping along the body of the boat and was quickly shimmying his way toward the back of the vessel.

She and Drew raced back down the staircase and

through the cabin, having to nudge their way past passengers crowding the aisles and milling about the snack area.

Why weren't they in their seats? "Out of the way!" Sami shouted.

She hopped over a toddler on the floor. When she reached the stairwell leading to the back observation deck, she slowed, put her hand on her holstered sidearm and proceeded up the steps with caution. Drew came up behind her.

"Easy, now," he whispered.

She nodded and stepped out onto the deck, prepared to defend herself. Several people took advantage of the open space, most of them taking a smoke break. The scent of tobacco drifted past Sami's nose and her stomach roiled. But the red-haired man wasn't among the smokers.

Drew moved past her to the side of the boat. He turned around and shook his head.

Her gaze moved to the two large metal storage bins that held travelers' luggage. Was the assailant hiding behind them? She gestured to Drew. He acknowledged her thought with a sharp nod, then stalked toward the containers. Sami took the left side, while Drew came around the right.

They found no one. However, her gaze snagged on red fibers sticking out from between the bins. Gingerly, she picked up a bright red wig. She'd been right. Clown hair. Beneath the wig was an army-green jacket. She spun around to study the ferry passengers, looking for signs of the assailant.

That was when she noticed the water tracks leading across the deck and down the other set of stairs going back inside the cabin.

Drew stopped at her side. She set the wig down and pointed to the droplets. "He has wet shoes and probably wet pant legs from dangling in the water."

Drew nodded and followed Sami into the main cabin, where they halted. There were at least two hundred people aboard the ferry. At least half of them were men.

"His eyes are blue this time," she told Drew.

Drew gave a short nod. "Stay to the left."

Sami slowly made her way down the aisle on the left side of the center row of seats while Drew took the right aisle. She kept alert for wet shoes, wet pants or anything else that could help her identify the blue-eyed attacker.

They both made it to the back of the ship without finding the assailant. Her head pounded, accentuating her frustration. "Could he have jumped overboard after all?"

"Doubtful," Drew countered. "Bathroom?"

"Worth a try." Wielding her badge, Sami shooed away the people in line and they each took a position alongside the door to the men's bathroom, her hand on her holstered weapon.

Drew banged on the metal portal. "Come out."

When no one responded, he flung the unlocked door open. Empty.

They turned their attention to the women's restroom. Drew tried the handle. Locked. He rapped his fist on the door commanding the occupant to come out. A moment later the door swung open and a teenage girl stood blinking at them. "What'd I do?"

"Sorry," Sami muttered, and stepped past the girl to stand next to Drew.

"Where could he be?" A chill skated over her flesh as

she again turned her attention to the passengers. Where was Birdman?

"He's on the boat somewhere. He didn't just vanish into thin air," Drew stated. "Let's talk to the captain."

They worked their way to the bridge, which was up a steep flight of stairs at the very top of the boat. A large window wrapped around the front of the bridge, providing the captain an unobstructed view of the sound.

There were three men on the bridge, including the captain, an older man with a head of silver hair, who stood in front of a sophisticated navigation system. The other two stood talking near an old-fashioned steering wheel in the middle of the bridge. A nice decoration, she knew, but no longer a useful tool.

One of the crew members turned toward them, blocking the way. "Passengers are not allowed up here."

"How about RCMP and FBI?" Drew said, showing the man his badge. Sami did the same.

"Of course." The man backed down. "How can I help?"

"Has anyone else come up here, say within the past few minutes?" Sami asked.

All three men shook their heads.

Sami looked at Drew. "How did we miss him?"

A muscle ticked in his jaw. "I don't know. But you're staying up here until we dock in Seattle."

"Not likely," Sami huffed. "*Our* job is to capture this maniac."

She wasn't going to be confined to the bridge as if she were helpless. She took out her phone and called the local FBI field office. They promised to meet the ferry at the dock. She hoped that Birdman wouldn't be able to slip away. They headed back down to the main cabin to continue their search.

* * *

When they docked in Seattle, she couldn't get off the ferry fast enough. The salty air felt good on her face and having steady ground beneath her feet helped combat the seasickness that still churned through her stomach. The FBI field agents had been at the customs intake gate, verifying passengers' IDs and tickets as they made their way off the boat.

Everyone checked out, much to Sami's frustration. They compiled a list of passengers, though, so instead of a one-in-a-billion chance of finding Birdman, they had it down to under one in three hundred. Better odds. But it would still take time to verify each ID. Keeping a copy of the passenger list for herself, she also had one sent to Jordon.

A local FBI field agent named Malcolm Talbot picked them up from the dock. They drove through a fast-food joint, but Sami could stomach only a soda, while Drew ate a hamburger. Then Talbot drove them to Virginia Mason Hospital.

The hospital complex sat on a hill overlooking the downtown cityscape. Afternoon sunlight glinted off the glass buildings. Overhead a clear blue sky belied the dark clouds hanging over her.

Agent Talbot stayed outside with the SUV while Sami and Drew entered through the main lobby doors. Sami was hit with a wave of fresh nausea as she inhaled the antiseptic smell that seemed to be common to all hospitals.

She knew it was whatever cleaning solution the hospital used but it stirred up the memories of when Ian had been shot and put her off hospitals for good. She clamped her mouth shut and willed her insides to calm while focusing on the task at hand.

One side of his mouth lifted in a half smile.

Her pulse jumped. It was disconcerting how easily he affected her. Working to calm herself, she squared her shoulders and lifted her head as they approached the admission desk, showed the attendant their badges and asked to speak with Lonnie Freeman. The attendant directed them to the Jones Pavilion, the next building over, where Lonnie worked in the critical care unit.

"You okay?" Drew asked as they left the main hospital and headed for the sliding door on the newer building.

"I don't like hospitals," she said.

"Who does?" he quipped.

"But I *really* don't like them."

He gave her an assessing look, the investigative wheels in his head turning. He was good at his job and she feared he'd ask for details, so she made a show of checking the directory on the wall inside the doors.

The critical care unit was located on level nine. They took the elevator up and stepped into a world of soft beige walls and white counters, hushed voices and the distinctive beeping sounds of monitors.

At the desk, they again showed their badges and asked to speak to Lonnie Freeman.

"I'll see if she's available," the woman behind the counter said. "Please have a seat in the waiting area."

They waited for five minutes before a silver-haired woman in blue scrubs approached. "I'm Lonnie Freeman. Can I help you?"

When they made their introductions, surprise widened Lonnie's dark eyes. "Is there a problem?"

"We have some questions about your sister's murder," Drew said.

Lonnie narrowed her gaze. "Why now? It's been thirty years. The last time I checked with the Victoria police, the case was still cold. Chief Heyes didn't hold out any hope that her killer would be found."

"Is there somewhere private we can speak?" Sami asked.

Lonnie nodded and led them to an unexpected courtyard overlooking the cityscape. She sat on a stone bench. "Are you reopening my sister's case?"

Sami sat next to her. "In a way. We believe that the person who killed your sister might be the same person we're looking for now."

Lonnie's eyebrows rose. "I don't understand. How do you know it's the same man?"

"We don't for sure," Drew said. He stood next to Sami. His stance appeared relaxed but Sami could feel the tension emanating from his body.

"But there's been another murder like Becca's," Lonnie said. It wasn't a question. She ran her palms along the tops of her thighs.

Sami exchanged a glance with Drew. There was a fine balance of how much they should or could reveal. But in order to gain Lonnie's trust and cooperation, Sami felt they needed to divulge at least that much. "Yes. We really want to catch this guy."

"How can I help you? I wasn't there."

"But Becca's son was," Sami said. "We were hoping you could put us in touch with him."

Lonnie shook her head. Sadness filled her face. "Corben doesn't remember anything from that night. He didn't talk for a solid three years after the murder.

And even after he finally regained his will to speak, it was another ten years of intense therapy before he stopped having nightmares."

"Nightmares suggest he saw something," Sami pointed out. She should know. She had her fair share of night terrors reliving the moment Ian was shot.

"Maybe," Lonnie said. Her mouth twisted and anger flashed in her eyes. "My sister wasn't a good mother. She abused that poor boy. He has scars all over his body from her abuse."

Empathy knotted inside Sami. Child abuse set her teeth on edge and ignited a deep fire in the pit of her stomach.

"Where is Corben now?" Drew asked.

"Working, I suppose," Lonnie said. "He's a pilot for Cloud Jet Airlines and also flies for a private company."

They'd flown on Cloud Jet from Portland to Vancouver Island. Sami's heart thumped and her gaze jumped to Drew's. Could Corben Kraft be the killer they were looking for?

TEN

"A pilot?" Drew asked, needing to confirm what he'd just heard Lonnie say regarding her nephew, Corben. A pounding began in Drew's head that competed with the sound of traffic from the nearby Seattle freeway echoing off the outside walls of Virginia Mason Hospital and swirling through the courtyard where they stood.

Lonnie nodded. "He joined the air force when he graduated from high school. He missed the Gulf War and was out before the Iraq war. But he served his country and was able to move right into a job with the airline," Lonnie said with obvious pride in her voice.

"Which hub city does he fly out of?" Sami asked. Her voice, though modulated, couldn't hide the vibration of anticipation.

"Here at Sea-Tac."

"You said he also flies planes for a private company?"

"Yes. The Smithen Group. Several businessmen banded together and bought a jet. They have six pilots on retainer. They rotate as they are available. Corben says they pay well." Lonnie frowned. "Please don't go dredging up Becca's murder. Corben has been doing so good."

"You mentioned he was in therapy," Sami said. "Can you tell us the name of the doctor?"

"Dr. Cantwell. She has an office in the administration center across the freeway," Lonnie said. "Through art therapy she was able to coax Corben out of his shell. She worked wonders with him."

They needed to talk to Dr. Cantwell. "You said Corben is based here in Seattle. Does he live with you?" Drew asked.

"No, he shares a house with coworkers in Renton. A nearby suburb."

"Do you have a picture of your nephew?" Sami asked.

She shook her head. "Not on me."

"What can you tell us about Corben's father?" Drew asked.

Lonnie's mouth twisted. "Becca wouldn't talk about him. I half suspect she didn't know who he was. She wasn't very discriminating in her love life." Lonnie looked at her watch. "I really need to get back on the floor."

"We understand," Drew said. "One last question. Why did your sister take Corben to Victoria?"

Lonnie sighed. "I have no idea. We hadn't spoken to each other in years. She moved to the Midwest after our parents passed on. I assume they were there on vacation. That's what the police told me. Now, I really must go." She hurried back inside the hospital.

"I'm texting Jordon now," Sami said. "He'll track down Corben's address in Renton and pull his DMV records and pilot's credentials."

Drew checked the passenger manifest for Corben's name. It wasn't on the list. Though as wily as Birdman appeared to be, Drew figured that if Corben was their guy, he most likely had a fake ID to use when committing his crimes.

They walked back into the hospital and stopped at the admitting desk. The helpful volunteer manning the desk gave them directions to the building where they would find Dr. Cantwell. Agent Talbot drove them the short half mile to the Virginia Mason Seattle Administration Center. Sami led the way up the stairs to Dr. Cantwell's office on the fifth floor.

They quickly found the correct office and entered into a calming blue-and-brown-toned waiting area with comfortable faux-leather chairs and couches. A woman sat behind a partition with a sliding Plexiglas window. A closed door to the right of the reception desk was closed and a sign on the door read In Session.

There were two people waiting. An older man who appeared to be sleeping and a middle-aged woman reading a magazine.

The receptionist smiled as they approached. "Can I help you?"

Drew showed his badge.

Sami did the same. "We need a moment with the doctor."

The woman's eyes widened. "She's in session. I can't disturb her unless it's an emergency."

"How long until she's available?" Drew asked.

"This client's time will be up in ten minutes, but Dr. Cantwell has a full schedule and doesn't like to get behind."

"Too bad. We'll wait ten minutes and no more," Sami stated. "And for the record, this *is* an urgent matter."

The woman nodded. "I'll send the doctor a quick

note." Her fingers went to the keyboard of the computer at her side.

Drew sat while Sami paced. He could see the jumble of thoughts playing through her mind. Her face was easy to read. Obviously, she was excited at the prospect of finding Corben and pinning the murders on him. Drew didn't begrudge her the need for closure on her friend's brutal death.

Yet Sami was a good investigator and knew they didn't have enough facts to support their theory that Corben Kraft was indeed Birdman. They needed more than a hunch that Birdman managed to cross the international border as an airline pilot.

Exactly ten minutes later the doctor's office door opened. A teenage girl walked out, her eyes downcast. The woman in the waiting area set aside the magazine, rose and put an arm around the girl. Together they left. Drew wondered what trauma had made the girl seek therapy.

"You may go in," the receptionist said.

Sami didn't waste any time; she stalked toward the door. Drew followed, putting his hand at the small of her back as they entered the office. They found the good doctor seated behind a large mahogany desk fronted by two leather chairs. Drew gauged the doctor's age to be early sixties. Streaks of gray had invaded her dark hair, which was held back by a clip. She had cool green eyes and a polite smile.

She rose but kept her fingers clasped together in front of her. "I'm Dr. Cantwell. Jenny tells me you have an urgent matter you wish to discuss."

Sami showed her badge. "I'm Special Agent Bennett, and this is RCMP Inspector Kelley."

Dr. Cantwell inclined her head in acknowledgment. "Please, have a seat." She sat and indicated the two chairs.

"We have some questions regarding one of your patients. Corben Kraft," Sami said.

The doctor's brows puckered ever so slightly. "You do know that doctor-patient privilege precludes me from discussing any patient without the patient's written consent. HIPAA and all that."

"We understand," Drew said. The Health Insurance Portability and Accountability Act provided privacy protection to US citizens just as the Health Information Protection Act protected Canadian citizens. "We just need some general questions answered, nothing that would violate any laws."

Dr. Cantwell gave him a small smile. "I'm sure you believe that and maybe in Canada things work differently, but here there is very little I can say."

"Can you confirm that Corben Kraft is your patient?" Sami pressed.

Steepling her hands, Dr. Cantwell regarded Sami with evident curiosity. "What do the FBI and—" she turned her gaze to Drew "—the Royal Canadian Mounted Police want with Corben?"

"We're reopening the murder of his mother," Sami said.

Drew slanted her a glance and kept the surprise from his expression. He wasn't sure he'd have played that card just yet. But he'd come to trust Sami's judgment. He turned his focus on the doctor to assess her reaction.

Surprise crossed Dr. Cantwell's face. "Really?" She sat back. "Well, that is interesting."

"How so?" Drew asked.

Again she sent him that small smile as if he were an errant child who needed schooling. "I'm sure the police report stated that Corben was deeply traumatized by the violent nature of his mother's death."

"Yes," Sami confirmed. "We spoke with his aunt, who became his guardian."

"Lonnie," Dr. Cantwell said. "Such a nice woman."

"When did you stop seeing Corben?" Sami asked.

Dr. Cantwell's eyebrows rose. "What makes you think he stopped coming to see me?"

Slick. Though the doctor didn't answer the question directly, she revealed that Corben was still under her care. Did she know something about Corben that she wanted to tell them but was prevented from saying by the law and her Hippocratic oath?

"Lonnie said that art therapy helped Corben. What exactly is art therapy?" Sami asked.

"Art therapy combines psychotherapeutic practices with creativity and artistic methods to improve mental health and well-being." She gestured to the corner of the office at a table cluttered with art material—paints, brushes, drawing pencils and pads of various sizes. Even modeling clay.

"I use a variety of art media to help children and adults process a wide spectrum of mental and physical issues. The purpose is to have the patient express their internal images, feelings, thoughts and ideas," Dr. Cantwell explained.

"What sort of images did Corben express?" Sami asked. She sat on the edge of her seat, nearly bouncing with pent-up energy.

Dr. Cantwell reached for a large leather-bound book on the shelf behind her. "I keep a portfolio of my patients' work. With their permission, of course. It helps demonstrate the type of therapy I do for new clients." She flipped open the book and turned several pages before landing on one. She spun the book so they could look at the open page from the correct perspective.

Drew heard Sami's sharp intake of breath. His own breath stalled as he stared at the crude drawing of a bird. A bird like the ones Birdman used as his signature at the crime scenes of the women he'd murdered.

"Do you know the significance of the bird?" Drew asked.

Dr. Cantwell shook her head. "No, I don't."

Sami took the book to look closer at the drawing. "Corben never told you why he drew this bird?"

"Draws birds," the doctor said softly.

Drew took her words to mean Corben was still drawing birds. Did the doctor know what Corben had been up to recently? If he'd confided in her, that he intended to kill, she'd be criminally remiss in not reporting it. But if he hadn't revealed his intent, then she had to keep his sessions with her confidential.

Dr. Cantwell sat back and regarded them with interest in her expression. "There's more going on than reopening a thirty-year-old cold case, isn't there?"

Sami lifted her gaze to Drew. He could read the question in her blue eyes. Did they confide in the doctor in hopes she'd cooperate and give them information that could help bring Corben to justice?

He nodded at Sami's unspoken question. Corben already knew they were onto him. He'd tried to kill Sami three times. They needed a break in this case, and if the doctor could provide some help, then they had to tell her what was at stake.

Sami turned to the doctor. "Corben Kraft is a person of interest in a string of murders."

Drew watched Dr. Cantwell closely for some sign of surprise. The woman's face went completely blank. She blinked several times as if processing the information Sami had just divulged. She did know something.

"Do you have proof?" Dr. Cantwell asked.

Sami held up the drawing in the book. "The killer leaves bird drawings exactly like this one at the crime scenes."

The doctor sat up. "Really? That is curious." Her gaze narrowed. "You will need a judge's order for me to hand over the files you want to see."

The subtle meaning behind her words wasn't lost on Drew. The doctor wanted them to see Corben's file, but she also had to protect the integrity of her practice.

"We'll get one," Sami said.

"Please come back when you do." Dr. Cantwell rose, her expression troubled. "Now, my other patients are waiting. Good day, officers."

Sami set the book on the desk.

As they left, Drew cast a glance over his shoulder. The crude bird depicted on the page seemed to mock them.

"A judge's order will take a couple of hours," Sami said after hanging up with her boss. "Until then let's concentrate on Corben."

They were seated in the black SUV with Agent Talbot at the wheel. He started the engine. "Do you have an address?"

Sami checked her phone. Sure enough, Jordon had found Corben Kraft's Renton address. Agent Talbot plugged it into the SUV's navigation system and then they were off, weaving through Seattle's congested freeways.

Jordon had also sent Corben's driver's license photo. The man in the picture bore a resemblance to her attacker but she couldn't be sure until they picked Corben up. Though height and weight were close to what she remembered, the DMV listed his hair color as blond, his eyes as gray.

They arrived at a white two-story single-family home in a residential neighborhood bordered by a park and a middle school. The front lawn was brown and the shrubs overgrown. Sami was sure the neighbors weren't too happy with the lack of yard care.

Talbot brought the vehicle to a halt. They got out and filed up the walkway to the front door with Drew leading the trio. Once they were on the porch, Sami stepped next to him, shoulder to shoulder. Well, almost. She liked that he was taller than her. She also liked how well they worked together, as if they'd been partnered forever rather than a few days.

Talbot took up a rear position to watch their backs as Drew rang the bell. A few seconds later the door opened and a tall man wearing a pilot's uniform greeted them.

"Hello. Can I help you?" He had dark graying hair and a mustache, both of which looked very real. He was not the man who'd attacked her on the ferry.

"We need to speak with Corben Kraft," she said briskly as she held up her identification.

Surprise widened the man's hazel eyes. "He's not here. I haven't seen Corben in months."

"Do you have ID?" Drew asked, beating Sami to the question.

She glanced at him, pleased that their thoughts were so in sync. A good thing in a partner. Would they be so compatible if they weren't in the middle of an investigation?

She mentally pushed that question aside. Letting herself go down that particular path wouldn't lead to some rosy romance. Better to remember he was her partner on a case, not a potential life mate.

The man reached into his back pocket and produced a leather wallet. He flipped it open to show his Washington State driver's license, which gave his name as Alec Delany.

"Corben doesn't live here?" Drew asked, returning to their reason for the visit.

Sami watched Alec closely to determine if the man was a liar or not.

"Oh, he does, when he's in town," Alec said.

Deciding Alec was telling the truth, she asked, "May we come in?" She wanted to see Corben's domain. Hopefully, they'd find something to lead them to him.

"Sure." The man stepped aside to allow them to enter. "What is this about?"

The inside of the house was better maintained than the outside, though the living room was sparsely furnished with only a couch, coffee table and a television. No pictures on the walls, no books on the table. Not even a throw pillow. Not very homey.

"We need to find Corben, Mr. Delany." Sami looked at the man expectantly. "Do you know where he goes when he's not working?"

Alec shook his head. "I barely know him."

"But you work with Corben?" Drew asked.

"You could say that, I guess." Alec frowned. "We

work for the same airline, but we don't pull the same shifts. And he has a second job that often takes him out of town."

Noticing different sizes of shoes on a rack inside the entryway, Sami asked, "How many people live in the house?"

Alec gave her a half smile. "Well, that depends on the day. Several pilots use the house as a crash pad between flights. Corben owns the house, so he has the master bedroom, which is off-limits to the rest of us. I rent one of the upstairs bedrooms. The other two bedrooms have a revolving door."

"Interesting." And weird. Sami didn't like the idea of people coming and going. "Is there anyone else on the premises?"

"Nope, just me today. I have a twenty-four-hour layover before I fly back out."

"So where does Corben stay when he's not here?" Drew asked.

Alec shrugged. "Beats me. Like I said, I don't know him very well."

"When was the last time you saw him?" Drew asked.

Alec thought for a moment. "Around Mother's Day. Has he done something wrong?"

"We have some questions for him," Sami hedged, not willing to reveal what they suspected. Who knew, maybe this Alec character was in on the murders. Maybe Birdman did have accomplices. She made a mental note to have Jordon dig into Alec Delany's background. "You wouldn't happen to have a picture of Corben, would you?"

Shaking his head, Alec replied, "No. He's kind of

funny about cameras. Gets really upset if anyone tries to take his picture. He's a bit of an odd duck."

"How so?" Drew asked.

"He doesn't talk much," Alec said. "Keeps to himself when he's here. And from what I've heard the others say, he's not a joy to work with. No personality, you know. If you're copiloting with him, be prepared to work in silence."

"Can you show us his room?" Sami asked.

"Uh, sure, I guess." Uncertainty crossed Alec's face. "Don't you need a search warrant or something?"

Sami ground her teeth but she fought to keep her frustration out of her tone. "Are you refusing? Makes me think you have something to hide."

Alec tucked in his chin. "Me? No, nothing to hide. Though I should contact Corben and get his permission before letting you into his room."

"You have a way of contacting him?" Drew asked, his voice sharp. "We need that information."

"I have his cell phone number." Alec fished his phone out of a briefcase on the dining room table. He scrolled through and found the number.

Sami placed her hand over Alec's, stopping him before he could push the dial button. "We need that number."

Alec relinquished the phone. She handed it off to Agent Talbot. "Find out if Kraft's phone is on and get a location on him."

Talbot nodded and took the phone outside.

"Hey, I need that," Alec protested.

"You'll get it back," Sami promised. "Look, we're up against a ticking clock. A man's life is at stake." At least she hoped James Clark was still alive but she wasn't holding her breath with hope. "It would be so much better for you if you cooperate and let us peek into Corben's room. You wouldn't want to obstruct justice, would you?"

"Of course not." Alec pointed toward the kitchen. "His suite is on the other side of the kitchen."

"Thank you," she said, and slipped past him with Drew on her heels.

They passed through the clean though outdated kitchen with worn linoleum and chipped pea-green laminate countertops. A short hallway led to a closed door. She paused outside the door. Alec said he hadn't seen Corben in months but that didn't mean their suspect couldn't be inside that room.

If it had indeed been Corben who'd tried to push her over the ferry railing, then he could very well have come home and could be waiting for them.

With her hand on the butt of her holstered weapon, Sami turned the knob and swung the door open. The large master bedroom was crowded with boxes stacked in every corner. A queen-size bed was topped with books and art supplies. Clothes were strewn across the floor, making Sami think of what her bedroom had looked like when she was a teenager.

Drew checked the adjacent bathroom. "Clear."

Pulling on a pair of gloves, Sami walked to the bed and inspected the paints, brushes and colored pencils. She found a box marked Stamps. She opened the lid to reveal several ink pads and a collection of rubber stamps in various sizes. All of the stamps had the same exact bird image. A label on the lid of one ink pad gave the name of a company.

Obviously, Corben had uploaded his crude drawing

and had custom stamps made of it. Another box had custom-made stickers with the same bird image. There was a stack of drawing pads, as well.

Sami knew what she'd find even as she opened the top pad. More images of the same bird.

Why this bird? Why did Corben draw only the same bird over and over again?

The edge of an envelope peeked out from between the stacks of drawing books. Gingerly, she slid the letter-sized plain white envelope out and opened it. Inside was a folded piece of paper. Carefully, she opened the sheet.

The words scrawled across the page in red pencil screamed at her.

"Special Agent Samantha Bennett, how clever are you?"

She gasped as the implications ran through her mind. Corben had known she'd find him and this place eventually.

How long ago had he written it? Had he followed them to his aunt's workplace? To his doctor's?

Or was this a trap? She needed to warn Drew and Talbot. "Drew!"

"Sami, you need to see this," Drew called from inside the walk-in closet.

Holding the sheet of paper by the edge, Sami hurried to the closet and halted abruptly.

There were no clothes hanging from the rods, no shoes lined up along the floor. Instead the closet was some sort of shrine to Birdman's madness. The sides of the walls in the small tight space were covered with more bird images and photos.

Corben had documented his killing spree.

Though she stood on solid ground, her stomach roiled as if the world had suddenly shifted.

Drew faced her and stepped closer, putting his hands on her shoulders. "Take a deep breath."

She stared at his concerned face, focusing on him rather than the panic creeping over her, and did as he instructed. Then slowly, he turned her around while still holding on to her shoulders.

Her gaze landed on a collage of photos on the back wall of the closet.

Photos of her.

ELEVEN

Sami's face stared back at her from a multitude of images. Icy dismay filled her veins. This was not a trap. It was a taunt.

Her hand convulsed, crumpling the note. Her mind reeled as she took in the pictures showing her going into her home, coming out of her home. At the grocery store, at the bank. Going into the FBI building in Portland.

There were pictures of her at the various crime scenes she'd visited during her investigation into Birdman.

Her breath caught when she realized that several of the photos were from before Lisa's death.

Her knees buckled. If Drew hadn't been holding on to her, she'd have gone down for sure. She was grateful for his rock-solid presence.

If she'd had to face this alone… Thankfully, she didn't. She had a partner. And as much as she'd been wary of taking on another partner after what happened to Ian, she was extremely grateful for Drew.

Pointing to one picture, she told Drew, "This was from Thanksgiving of last year." A shudder worked its way over her. "Lisa wasn't killed until January."

"How often have you flown on Cloud Jet Airlines?"

Dawning horror flooded through her, filling her lungs and making her gasp for air. "Several times," she whispered. "Before the recent flights, last November I flew to Atlanta for a symposium on—" Her voice faltered. A deep pain engulfed her, nearly drowning her in its intensity. "Oh, no. Did Corben kill Lisa to get my attention?"

The thought chilled her to the bone. Guilt ate at her insides. Tears burned the back of her eyes. *Oh, Lisa, I'm so sorry.*

But why would he want her attention? Why her?

"What was the symposium on?" Drew asked gently as his hold on her tightened. She leaned against him, absorbing his strength because at the moment hers had abandoned her.

"Serial murder." She clamped a hand over her mouth as her stomach heaved but there was nothing in her to expel.

Drew turned her around. The concern etched on his handsome face made her want to slip her arms around him and hang on for dear life. But she didn't. She had to be strong, brave. For Lisa. For all the victims.

"Lisa's death is not your fault," he said passionately. "None of this is your fault."

"He must've been there," she said. "We need to see if there's an unsolved murder in Atlanta. He must have been laughing at us, the big bad FBI agents converging on a hotel to discuss serial killers while he was roaming around free to take lives."

"You found him," Drew said.

"But he's still out there."

"Not for long." Drew led her out of the closet. "We need to get the crime scene people here."

"There's more." She handed him the wrinkled sheet of paper. Her hand shook.

Drew took the note and shook his head. "Smug, isn't he?"

For some reason Drew's reaction made her smile. He wasn't intimidated or freaked out by Birdman. Good. Because they had a battle ahead of them. They'd come so close, failed so many times. They had to find a way to capture him.

Drew slipped an arm around her shoulders. She put her arm about his waist and allowed herself a moment to lean on him. She was so tired she didn't know how much longer she could go on.

After a moment she disengaged and they stepped into the living room, where Agent Talbot had kept an eye on Alec in case the man decided to run.

"This is officially a crime scene," Drew announced briskly. "Mr. Delany, you'll need to step outside."

They went out of the house and Sami searched for any sign of Corben watching her. As he apparently had been doing for some time now. She shuddered with revulsion. She couldn't wait to see the menace put behind bars for the rest of his miserable life.

"Agent Talbot, anything on Kraft's cell phone?" Drew asked.

"He must have turned it off. Our tech is monitoring the number in case he turns it back on," Talbot said. "The last incoming call was from the airline. No outgoing calls at all."

"Too bad," Drew said. "We need a CSI team to process the house."

"Also contact the airlines and something called The Smithen Group," Sami added. "We need Corben's flight schedules for both entities going back to when he first was hired by both the airline and the private corporation."

Talbot nodded, then stepped aside to make the necessary arrangements.

Sami phoned Special Agent in Charge Granger to fill him in on what they'd found in Corben's house. As she spoke, she sank down on the curb, her legs no longer willing to hold her up.

"A closet full of photos of you?" Granger growled. She could picture his jaw hardening and his eyes narrowing to slits as they always did when he was angry. "Okay, that's it. I'm pulling you off this case. You need to return here where we can protect you."

Her stomach dropped. "No, sir, please. I'm so close to catching him."

"He's obviously obsessed with you."

She couldn't deny that fact. "I can't stop now. I have to see this through."

After a moment of tense silence, Granger said, "I want you formally under protection, Agent Bennett."

Though the words chafed, she wouldn't argue, not if it meant she could stay active on the case. She sought out Drew, who stood a few paces away on his phone, no doubt talking to his boss or the IBETs team.

She thought of the many ways Drew had been there for her. He'd comforted her, strengthened her, even sacrificed his own body to shield her from the flying shrapnel that had once been her house. Affection for the man spread through her chest. She was glad to have him on her side, and in her life. "I know the perfect person for the job. Inspector Kelley is a tough man to shake."

Granger grunted. Sami took that as approval.

"Find out when Kraft's next flight is," Granger instructed. "Have airport security be on the lookout for him, too. Get the local police involved, as well. If they can detain him before he gets to the plane, that would be optimum. And the less the public knows about this, the better. We don't need to stir up a media circus."

"On it, sir."

"And, Samantha…" Granger's voice took on a harsh note.

"Sir?"

"Be careful. I don't want to lose one of my best agents."

Warmed by his concern and the compliment, she promised she'd be cautious. She clicked off and immediately the phone rang. "Agent Bennett."

"Jordon here," came the tech's deep voice. "I found something interesting on Becca Kraft."

"Tell me."

"Her name is listed on the deed to a house in Michigan, just outside Detroit."

Sami's pulse jumped. Detroit. The city where Corben Kraft had killed for the first time. Twenty-eight years after his mother's unsolved murder.

Something niggled at the back of Sami's mind, like a shadow that disappeared every time she attempted to look at it.

"And get this," Jordon said, drawing her attention back to the conversation. "The house was never sold. The same corporation that originally purchased the house in Becca's name all those years ago still owns the house. It's been empty all these years."

Sami doubted that Corben hadn't visited the home he'd shared with his mother. "Text me the address."

Why hadn't Lonnie told them about the house in Michigan?

"Just did."

Within seconds a text came through with the address for Corben's childhood home.

Drew sat next to her, so close she could easily rest her head on his shoulder. His leg brushed hers when he stretched. Awareness rippled over her.

"Corben has another potential hideout," she told Drew, and tilted the phone so Drew could hear Jordon.

"And it gets better," Jordon continued. "The property taxes have been paid through a corporation. I'm working on tracking down the responsible party, but whoever set this up knew what they were doing. Plus, when the house was bought thirty-eight years ago, there were no computers, so I'm having to do some old-school investigating."

"I appreciate your effort. Hey, Jordon, can you check with Atlanta PD's cold case division? See if they have any similar crimes to our current ones dating back to November of last year?" She was checking on the location of the symposium.

"Will do. Anything else?"

"Not yet. Let me know when you find who owns the corporation." She clicked off.

"A dummy corporation," Drew mused. "Hmm. Curious. Who had been in Becca's life and would have provided for her?"

"Corben's father?" Sami suggested. "Lonnie had suspected Becca didn't know who fathered Corben. But maybe Becca had known."

"And that man could have set Becca and Corben up with a house. That's plausible." Drew gestured to his phone. "My people obtained a sample of James Clark's DNA. They're working with Portland Forensics to see if he's a match to the body part we found in your house."

"Good." Her mind turned over the possibilities. "If they are a match, then we'll have our answer as to whether James Clark is still alive."

Talbot joined them. "Corben deadheaded on a flight bound for JFK Airport in New York. Apparently airline employees can use unsold seats on their off time."

"He's running," Sami said. "We need to alert airport security and the New York field agents."

"Already done," Talbot said.

Sami rose. Holding out her hand to Drew, she said, "We need to find out why Lonnie forgot to mention the house in Michigan."

His hand clasped hers. The warmth of his palm and the pressure of his fingers curling overs hers sent delicious little sparks shooting up her arm. He stood but didn't release her hand.

"Seems odd that she'd let the house sit for so long unoccupied."

"Right." She stared at their joined hands. His was so much bigger, stronger. "Remind me what your people found out about James Clark."

"Married. Business owner. Two adult offspring. What are you thinking?"

"This is a long shot, but I can't stop thinking about the fact that Birdman switched gears. Going from all female victims to one random man. Maybe he wasn't so random?" She tugged on her bottom lip for a second, her mind working through the niggling detail that wanted her attention.

"You think Clark has some connection to Corben?" Drew stroked his chin with his free hand as he mulled that over. "Okay, I'll buy in. What's the connection?"

"I don't know yet. But think about it," Sami said. "Twenty-eight years after the murder of his mother, Corben kills his first victim."

"You're supposing he didn't kill his mother," Drew pointed out.

"True. I don't think he did. The brutal nature of the crime and the force necessary seems far beyond the capability of an eight-year-old boy. Even an abused boy who might have acted out of rage."

"Then what? You think James Clark murdered Becca Kraft and Corben exacted revenge on him thirty years later?"

"Why not?" The more she thought about it, the more it made sense.

"If that's the case, then why not start with Clark? Why kill so many women?"

"Practice? He wanted to make sure he could do it?" Sami said, grasping at possible motivations. "Though we won't know for sure until we have Corben in custody." She withdrew her hand from Drew's and pushed the button to call back Jordon. "I'll have my tech guy see what he can dig up on Clark. Maybe we can find out what he was really doing in the States."

Drew took out his phone, as well. "And I'll have my people check to see if Clark was in Victoria thirty years ago."

After hanging up with their respective teams, they joined Talbot as he hung up with the New York FBI field office. "Security has been alerted in New York City and in the airport. When the plane lands, they'll nab Corben Kraft."

"Good." Tension drained from Sami's body. Though she was still alert, she didn't think she needed a bodyguard. Neither was she ready to let Drew go. They still had work to do, a case to solve. "Let's go talk to Lonnie again."

When they arrived at the hospital, they were told Lonnie had gone home sick. Getting her address took another ten minutes. Lonnie lived in an apartment in Redmond, Washington, beneath the shadow of Microsoft, Nintendo and over three hundred other technology companies. A tech fanatic's paradise.

After a half hour of working their way through Seattle's commuter traffic to the suburb east of the metropolitan area, they drove into downtown Redmond and quickly found the apartment complex. It was a four-story eighteen-unit boxy building set back in a wooded area off the main road. Sami led the way to Lonnie's apartment on the third floor.

The door was ajar. She halted, holding up her clenched fist to clue Drew and Talbot to stop. The fine hairs at the back of her neck rose and caution blanketed her like a mist. With one hand on the butt of her holstered weapon, she approached the door and toed it open to reveal a narrow hallway.

"Lonnie?" she called out. "It's Agent Bennett."

No answer. Dread slithered across her skin. She met Drew's grim gaze.

She withdrew her sidearm and eased over the threshold into the dimly lit passageway. Leading with her gun, she checked the first open door and the large bathroom.

Empty. She continued until she came to the end of the hall, which opened to a large living space with floor-to-ceiling windows letting in the setting sun's rays. To her left a kitchen with standard appliances ran along one wall, while the right side of the studio held a futon situated in front of a television set.

With a start, Sami realized Lonnie was sitting on the futon, her back to them. Drew moved past Sami to open the sliding doors to the closet. No one was hiding inside.

"Lonnie." Keeping her weapon at the ready, Sami stepped around the end of the futon until she could face Lonnie. She sucked in a harsh breath.

Lonnie's head listed slightly to the side. Her eyes were open and showed petechial hemorrhaging. A thin dark bruise circled her neck above the collar of her scrubs.

Sami holstered her weapon, slid on a pair of gloves and checked Lonnie's pulse. She was dead. Sami didn't need a medical examiner to announce the cause of death. She'd been strangled. And the weapon, a computer cord, lay coiled on the floor like a snake ready to strike.

Another realization slammed into Sami and she snatched her hand back.

"She's still warm." Alarmed, she met Drew's gaze. Lonnie hadn't been dead long. "If Corben's on a plane to New York, then—" Her lungs seized, refusing to take in oxygen.

"Then Birdman has a partner. And he's on the loose." Drew finished her thought. His grim voice matched the expression on his face.

The ramifications sliced through her. She still wasn't

safe. No one was safe. "Uh, so I told my boss you would act as my, uh, bodyguard until this was over."

Drew's expression softened. "You don't have to ask. And I'm honored. I know accepting protection is hard for you."

It dawned on her how well he'd come to know her in such a short time. The knowledge was alarming and yet made her feel cared for, special.

But it didn't matter how she felt. She'd made a gross error. "I failed Lonnie." Disappointment bowed her shoulders. "How could I have been so wrong?"

Drew pulled her close, wrapping her in a soothing cocoon. "Don't. There was no way *we* could've known she would be a victim."

She rested her forehead against his chest. "But why?" She fisted her hands. A hot fury flushed through her. "Why would Corben allow this? She loved him. It doesn't make sense."

"We can't hope to know the mind of a psychopath."

She straightened and couldn't keep the venom she felt from invading her voice. "I'd like to crawl inside his head and scramble his brains."

Drew smiled and the impact was like a cooling spray of spring water on the hot fire of her anger. "Maybe you can when the New York federal agents pick him up."

"Yeah." Sami wasn't sure she'd get the opportunity to interview Corben. Now that the brass had taken an interest in him, the higher-ups would do the heavy lifting. "Do you think Corben's partner was afraid Lonnie would point us in his direction?"

"Or hers."

"Right. Could be a woman." She sighed and looked around, realizing there were wooden photo frames turned upside down on the floor and broken pieces of glass glinting in the sun. She adjusted her gloves and picked up a frame. The picture had been taken out. She checked the other frames. "They're all empty."

"The partner protecting Corben."

"Or him or herself."

Talbot walked in. "Local police are here. Our forensic team is on their way."

Sami nodded her thanks. "Where are we on obtaining a judge's order for Dr. Cantwell's file on Corben Kraft?"

"I'll check on it." Talbot headed back outside, already on his cell.

"It's good to have minions," Sami remarked drily.

"It's good to work with a team," Drew replied.

She met his clear dark eyes, hit once again by the force of her trust in him. "True."

It was good to work with him. But she couldn't let herself get too used to having him around. The warm, almost heady feeling he gave her drained away. This partnership was temporary, she reminded herself, and for a single goal—to stop Birdman.

Once Corben Kraft and his partner were behind bars, Drew would return to his life and his work with IBETs, and she'd move on to the next case. Without Drew.

Purposely, she turned away from Drew and made a slow search of the studio apartment, looking for anything that might help them to understand Corben and why he, or his partner, had wanted Lonnie dead.

She paused at the desk in the corner where a computer monitor took up most of the space on the desktop. Next to it was a raised platform where a laptop would sit, acting like a desktop computer. The platform was empty. "The killer took her computer."

"More pictures?"

"Possibly. Or information on the dummy corporation that provided a home for Becca and her son."

"You think Lonnie was involved?" Drew stared at her with a quizzical expression. "I didn't get the impression Lonnie was hiding anything."

"She had to have known about the house in Detroit, right?"

"Maybe. But if a dummy corporation bought it, then maybe Lonnie expected that the company had reclaimed the place."

"Could be." Her gaze slid back to Lonnie. Her heart ached at the loss. "We may never know."

Talbot returned. "An agent will meet us at Dr. Cantwell's office with a judge's order."

Drew headed toward the front door. "Let's see if the doctor can shed some light on the situation."

"What do you mean, the doctor left?" Sami's incredulous voice rose, rousing the interest of two of the three people waiting to see the doctor.

Drew did a quick assessment of the three people in the quiet waiting area. A family, he guessed. The husband glanced at his watch, clearly annoyed by the delay. The nervous mother darted a glance from her husband to her teenage son and back. The boy, probably about fifteen, sat slouched in the chair with earbuds clinging to his ears, the cord running to an electronic device tucked inside the pocket of his shirt. A bomb could go off and the kid wouldn't notice.

"She stepped out right after you left." The receptionist lowered her voice. "She said she'd be right back but she hasn't returned."

Drew focused on the receptionist. "Did she receive a phone call before she left?"

The receptionist shook her head. "Not through the office phone."

"But she has a private phone," Sami said. "We need that number."

The woman quickly wrote the doctor's private cell number on a sticky note and handed it over to Sami.

"We have a judge's order for Dr. Cantwell's file on Corben Kraft." Drew gestured to the FBI agent, who handed the order over to the receptionist.

"Uh, Dr. Cantwell would need to find it. She's very particular about her files," she said, clearly unnerved.

"We'll find the file," Sami said.

The receptionist rose. "I don't think Dr. Cantwell would want you in her office without her here."

"Doesn't matter with a judge's order." Sami opened the door to the office and went inside.

Drew followed. The office looked exactly as it had a few hours ago, except the doctor wasn't behind her desk.

"I'll take the filing cabinet. You check her desk," Sami said as she opened a file drawer marked with the letters *I-J-K*.

Drew moved to the desk and opened the large file drawers. He checked the names on the files. No Corben Kraft.

"It's not here," Sami said slamming the cabinet drawer closed.

"Not here either." Drew checked the shallow middle drawer to find a plethora of pens, paper clips and prescription pads. Something caught his eye. Using a pen, he pushed the pads aside. On the bottom of the drawer was a bird drawing.

"She must have taken it with her." Sami's frustration echoed in her words.

"Look at this." Drew made room for her to step beside him.

"That bird again." She shook her head. "What does it mean?"

"And how did it get here?" Drew shut the drawer. "I didn't peg Dr. Cantwell as homicidal but…"

"She could be Corben's cohort. I don't think it's coincidence that she disappeared after our visit."

"Right." Drew had a hard time wrapping his brain around the concept. "So after trying to kill you three times, Corben flees after following us from Victoria. He finds out we talked to his aunt."

"She could've called him," Sami stated. "We need to get Lonnie's phone records."

"So Lonnie calls Corben while we're talking to Dr. Cantwell."

Sami nodded. "Then while we're at Corben's house, Dr. Cantwell takes Corben to the airport, where he gets on a plane bound for New York, where he could hop on another plane to leave the country."

"And then Dr. Cantwell drives to Redmond and kills Lonnie?" Drew shook his head. "You've seen the traffic out there. How could she get from her office to Sea-Tac Airport and then Redmond in the amount of time it took us to search Corben's house?"

"Driving in the car pool lane?" Sami guessed. She shrugged. "Once we find her, we can ask her."

Drew stepped into the waiting area. "We need Dr. Cantwell's home address."

The receptionist bit her lip and regarded him with uncertainty. "I don't think the doctor would want me to give out her private address."

"We could charge you with obstruction of justice," Sami said, joining Drew. The threat was becoming her favorite shtick.

The receptionist hesitated a second or two, then nodded. On another sticky note, she wrote down the doctor's home address.

They left the doctor's office and headed to the Queen Anne neighborhood northwest of downtown Seattle. Traffic crawled up the tight streets of the hill that made up the popular and posh area. Talbot did his best to maneuver around cars but the sea of vehicles was thick. Drew took a page from Sami and tapped his foot impatiently, his tempo matching the drumming of her fingers on the door handle.

Finally they reached the doctor's residence, a Queen Anne–style home like most of the other houses from which the area took its name. The house sat perched on the side of the hill with spectacular views of Elliott Bay and the Puget Sound.

Drew whistled through his teeth. "Nice place."

"Worth a few million," Sami said as they stepped onto the wide wraparound porch.

Drew knocked. The house remained quiet. Eerily so.

Exchanging glances, they separated, going in opposite directions, peering into the house through the large windows. They worked together like a well-oiled machine. Words weren't necessary.

They met in the back of the house. There was no sign of anyone in the house, no car in the carport. Disappointment seeped through Drew but he refused to give in to hopelessness. God had led them this far; He'd lead them the rest of the way.

"Place looks empty," Sami commented. "But we'll have an agent sit on the house in case the doctor comes home. If she's Corben's accomplice, maybe she's running, as well."

"Perhaps the doctor left with Corben?" Drew's lip curled. "She's been treating him since he was eight." The professional, regal woman they'd met earlier that day came to mind. Drew shook his head. "I have a hard time envisioning Dr. Cantwell and Corben in a romantic tryst."

"Yeah, that seems unlikely but then again..." Sami shrugged. "Stranger things have happened."

TWELVE

An hour later Sami restlessly paced the office of the Seattle FBI's SAC—special agent in charge. Drew leaned on the edge of the desk and loosened his tie. Talbot and his SAC both stood near the large windows that looked out of the high-rise building, which sat on a corner, surrounded by similar structures. The sun was low on the horizon, casting long shadows across the blue-carpeted offices and making her aware of her exhaustion.

A sofa pushed up against one wall was tempting. She needed to rest, but there was still work to be done. She rubbed the temples of her aching head.

Talbot brought his SAC up-to-date on Corben and Dr. Cantwell. "We've got a BOLO out for Dr. Cantwell."

Which meant that all law enforcement agencies would be on the lookout for her. She wouldn't be able to board a plane or train or bus easily. And if she was traveling by car...well, the license number, make and model of her Mercedes-Benz were in the hands of every police officer, trooper and federal agent across the country, not to mention at all the border crossings.

Corben's plane was still in the air, winging its way

to New York and the waiting FBI agents. There was nothing left for Sami and Drew to do.

Except…Sami had an uneasy sense that it was all too easy.

"As slippery as Birdman, aka Corben Kraft, has been up to this point, why would he telegraph where to capture him?" Sami said aloud.

"And what's Dr. Cantwell's part in all of this?" Drew said.

Sami contemplated what Drew said. "I agree with you it seems highly unlikely that Dr. Cantwell and Corben are linked romantically."

"But that doesn't mean they can't both share an affinity for murder."

A shiver of dismay made goose pimples rise on Sami's arms. "Could the doctor have killed Lonnie Freeman? Why?"

Drew shook head, his expression perplexed. "And the missing computer. What's on it that's worth killing for?"

"And don't forget the house in Michigan," Sami stated. "Who paid for it?"

Sami blew out a breath that did nothing to relieve her tension. "I'll call Jordon." She plucked her phone from her pants pocket.

When he answered, she said, "Talk to me. Tell me you have a name for the person who paid for Becca's house."

"Sorry, not yet," Jordon said.

Discouraged, she sat on the suede sofa and sank into the comfortable cushions. "Bummer."

"However, I did find out something about James Clark."

"He's been found?" Sami couldn't stem the tide of

hope. If he was alive, then maybe he could tell them why Corben had his credit card.

"No, he's still missing. His company is in disarray. Seems Mr. Clark was the heart and soul of Jaybird Aviation."

The name slammed through Sami's brain. Jaybird. Ugh. More birds. Drew had mentioned Clark owned an aviation company but at the time the knowledge held no significance.

Now… Did the fact Clark owned an aviation firm tie into Corben being a pilot? Had Corben worked for James Clark?

No, Lonnie had said Corben went straight from the military to the airline. So was Clark a victim or an accomplice? "Tell me about his company."

"Jaybird Aviation specializes in the production and manufacturing of parts and accessories for the commercial and military aerospace industry. James inherited the company from his father. They've been in business since the mid-'50s."

"Why the name Jaybird?"

"According to their website, Jay was the father's name. Maybe he added the word *bird* because of the reference to flying. But the interesting thing is James took over for his father thirty-eight years ago."

"Around the same time that Becca Kraft's house was bought." Sami could see the dots starting to line up but they weren't fitting together yet. "There has to be a connection between Clark's company and the corporation that purchased and still pays for Becca's house in Michigan."

And a connection between James and Corben. Was James Clark Corben's father?

"If you're right about a connection, I haven't found it

yet," Jordon said. "You asked if I could find out if James Clark was in Victoria at the time of Becca Kraft's murder."

Her pulse sped up. "Was he?"

Drew pushed away from the desk and moved to sit beside her. At his questioning look, she pointed to the phone and said, "Jordon has information on Clark." Into the phone she said, "So was he in Victoria?"

She tilted the phone so Drew could hear the answer. He pressed his head next to hers. The scent of his after-shave teased her senses and distracted her from Jordon's answer. She mentally forced herself to listen.

"I can't confirm that he was in Victoria, but I found a rental agreement with his name on it for a vacation home on Vancouver Island for around the same time."

Sami mulled that over. "Was he with his wife?" His kids wouldn't have been born yet.

"I don't know. That'd be something your inspector could have his people ask Mrs. Clark."

"Thanks, Jordon. Let me know if you find out anything else." She hung up and quickly relayed the information about the Clarks' business to Drew.

"Let me get someone out to the Clark house to ask the wife about Victoria," Drew said, and used his cell to make the call.

When he was done, Sami said, "The house in Michigan bugs me. I want to go there. It could have answers for us."

Drew considered her for a moment. "All right. Let's do it."

Since the next available flight to Detroit was in the morning, they spent the night in a hotel by Sea-Tac Airport in separate but connected rooms. They shared a late meal, then retired to their rooms. Sami had asked if he'd mind keeping the connecting door open. He hadn't. Acting as her protector filled him with a sense of responsibility he'd never had before. Not that he thought Sami wasn't capable of defending herself, but he was glad to watch her back.

When the alarm went off the next morning, Drew and Sami grabbed a quick bite from the hotel's continental breakfast and then rushed to the airport terminal to catch their flight. By the time they arrived at Detroit Metropolitan Wayne County Airport, Drew's limbs were stiff from sitting for so long. His phone had died midflight, as well. He stopped at a kiosk in the airport and bought a car charger, which he plugged into the rental car.

He let Sami drive the thirty minutes to the house on Bloomington Drive in the Detroit suburb of Franklin. The sun was setting; the last few rays of light glinted off the house's numbers.

She brought the sedan to a halt on the curve of a cul-de-sac. The Kraft home was set off the road. It was an eyesore. Abandoned, uncared for. The shrubbery was overgrown and weeds had overtaken the tall grass. Windows were boarded up. The front porch sagged and the screen door hung off its hinges, making Drew think a good wind could send the metal and mesh door flying.

"Doesn't look like anyone has been here in a long time," Sami stated, opening her car door.

"I'm sure the neighbors are thrilled," Drew commented as he stepped out of the vehicle.

Compared to the more temperate weather of Seattle, Michigan was hot. But not nearly as hot as Arizona, for which Drew was thankful. He'd take a bit of humidity and high eighties over the blazing heat of the desert any day. But his cotton dress shirt still stuck to his skin. He rolled up the sleeves. Sami, however, appeared unperturbed by the weather.

She looked fresh in her flowered top and black utility pants tucked inside her boots. She'd twisted her hair up and secured it in back with a clip. He remembered the way all that blond hair had looked flowing over her shoulders. He wanted to pluck the clip out to let the strands dance free. Instead he put one hand on his weapon and used the other to bat away a bee.

Carefully picking their way through the knee-high grass, Drew and Sami reached the porch stairs.

"Watch your step," he cautioned. The wood groaned beneath his weight as he stepped onto the porch.

Sami's phone rang. She paused on the bottom step to answer. "Agent Bennett."

Drew tried the doorknob. It was unlocked. Caution tripped down his spine. He placed a hand on the butt of his gun. Figuring Sami would be right behind him in a moment, he pushed the door open. The house was dark inside because boards covered the windows. He had just crossed the threshold when a trapdoor in the floor beneath him gave way.

Stunned, his arms windmilling, searching for something to grab on to, he fell into inky blackness.

With her back to the house, Sami's jaw dropped. She couldn't have heard Agent Talbot correctly. "Wait! What? Corben Kraft wasn't on the airplane when it landed in New York? How can that be? Why wasn't I informed of this earlier?"

"We wanted to make sure he hadn't slipped through,"

the agent explained. "I did call you earlier but it went to voice mail."

Because she'd been on a plane and then hadn't checked her messages. She'd been too intent on reaching the house.

Talbot went on to tell her that apparently, Corben had hired someone to pose as him for a thousand dollars and a free flight to New York. Which meant Corben hadn't left Seattle. At least not the way they'd thought. Talbot assured her they had every available officer in the state of Washington looking for Corben.

Sami looked toward the house and frowned. Drew had gone inside without her.

"Keep me updated," she told the agent.

She jammed the phone into her pocket and carefully went up the porch stairs. Rage burned like acid in her gut. Corben had played them. She'd known it had been too easy. While they were laying a trap for him in New York, he was… She didn't know where he'd gone. Was he still in Seattle? Had he crossed the border and was now in Canada or headed south through Oregon and California to Mexico?

She could only hope God saw fit to give her the knowledge necessary to capture Birdman.

She paused at the front door of the abandoned house. The interior was pitch-black. A musty, moldy scent hit her in the face. She wrinkled her nose. This wouldn't be good for her allergies.

"Drew?" she called out.

Silence met her voice.

The fine hairs on the back of her neck rose. Caution sent her senses into overdrive. The absolute lack of noise ratcheted the creep factor to high. She certainly wouldn't go inside alone.

But Sami wasn't alone. Drew was here, somewhere in the house, and she wasn't going to let fear derail her from her training.

With one hand on her weapon, she stepped inside the house. The floor creaked beneath her feet. Through the light coming in from the open door at her back she could tell the house was empty. No furniture to bump into, nothing to trip over. But shadows concealed the corners of the wide room she guessed was the living room.

Where was Drew?

She ventured farther into the house and could just make out the darker outline of a hallway straight ahead. "Drew?"

A whisper of noise from behind her startled her. She whirled around just as the front door slammed shut, throwing her into complete darkness. No light came through the slats of the boarded-up windows.

Terror streaked through her. Immediately, she crouched, making herself less of a target. With shaking hands, she dug out her phone, intending to use the flashlight feature, but before she could turn it on, something knocked the phone from her hand. The device skittered away and so did she until her back hit the wall.

Her mind scrambled to comprehend what was happening even as muscle memory kicked in and she pulled her gun. An assailant hid in the dark. Corben? Dr. Cantwell?

What happened to Drew?

Her partner could be hurt. Or worse, dead. Bile burned her throat. The thought of losing another part-

ner twisted her heart. But her priority had to be eliminating the danger.

Still in a crouch and leading with a two-handed grip
on her gun, she moved slowly in the direction of what
she hoped was the front door. She mentally ticked off
the steps. The dark overwhelmed her, playing havoc
with her equilibrium. She bumped into something solid
and froze. Her pulse jumped. Not a wall, and there was
no furniture.

Panic jolted through her. She jumped away and
whipped around, looking for a target. But the blackness concealed the threat.

If it were Drew, he'd say something, right?

The scuff of a shoe on the wooden floor sounded as
loud as a gunshot.

"Drew?" she whispered. *Please, dear God, let Drew
be okay.*

She prayed nothing had happened to him…not only
because he was her partner, but because, she was forced
to acknowledge, she cared for the big Canadian. Maybe
could even let herself love him if given a chance.

Something touched her hair. She jumped sideways,
hesitant to fire until she located Drew. Her bullet could
find him by mistake.

The door. She had to find the door and get out. But
then what? Leave Drew inside? No, she couldn't do
that. But if she could open the door, light would reveal
the person lurking in the shadows and she could neu-
tralize the threat. She inched her way in the direction
of the door.

In the back of her mind, this all felt familiar. Like
something she'd seen in a movie or on television. Then
it came to her with a sinking sensation in her gut. Her

heart beat at a rapid clip, she struggled to breathe. If she weren't living this, she'd never believe it. They were playing out a scene from a popular thriller. Had the movie been the impetus that started Corben on his killing spree? Art becoming reality. "Corben, is that you?"

A snickering came from her right. She spun around.

"It's me." A singsong voice assaulted her from behind. "You are clever, Agent Bennett, as I knew you would be."

"What did you do with Drew?" she demanded, though her voice didn't hold as much threat as it did fear.

"Oh, you'll see soon enough."

The disembodied voice had moved. She homed in on the spot where she thought he was and fired.

The flash of the bullet leaving the gun momentarily blinded her. A hole appeared in a board covering the front window, letting in a stream of light. She searched the shadows for Corben.

A hard shove on her back sent her stumbling toward the front door. She used the momentum to keep going forward. Just as she reached for the doorknob, she heard a faint click and the floor beneath her disappeared.

She fell through an opening and landed with a jarring thud onto a dirt floor. Her gun bounced away. Pain exploded in her head and air rushed out of her lungs. She blinked back the dust her abrupt fall had kicked up, but it was too late. The hole above her head had closed.

She flipped to her hands and knees. Her gaze swept what was really little more than a crawl space. A single bare bulb hung from a cord, providing enough dim light for her to see a closed two-feet-by-two-feet door and two figures propped up against the wall, bound and gagged.

She ignored Dr. Cantwell and went directly to Drew.

Relief to see him alive flooded her and filled her heart. She retrieved her gun and rushed to his side. "Thank you, God."

Reaching for the duct tape stretched across his mouth, she said, "This is going to hurt."

He nodded.

Wincing on his behalf, she ripped the tape from his face.

He flinched, then worked his jaw a second before asking, "Are you okay? I heard gunfire."

"I am now that I've found you." She slipped her knife from her boot and made quick work of cutting the thick cord holding him captive. "What happened?"

"I fell through the same trapdoor you just did." He rose to a crouch since the low ceiling wouldn't allow him to stand. "He was waiting for me with a stun gun."

She noticed his empty holster. "He took your side-arm."

Grimly, Drew nodded. "Unfortunately."

She was glad Corben hadn't used it on her while he'd toyed with her in the dark. "What about your phone?"

He grimaced. "Charging in the car."

And hers was somewhere above them. So much for calling in backup.

Sami's gaze landed on Dr. Cantwell, bound and gagged with duct tape just as Drew had been, only she was unconscious. Sami scrabbled to her side, cut the cords binding her hands and feet, laid her out flat and then gently shook her. "Dr. Cantwell."

She didn't respond. Sami checked her pulse. Steady.

"She's out cold. He must have drugged her," Sami said.

Drew tried the door handle, but it was locked. "There has to be another way out of here."

She searched along the walls for another exit. Drew worked at opening the trapdoor. She came up empty, and apparently so did Drew, if his frustrated growl was any indication.

Taunting laughter invaded the room. Sami's gaze went to the ceiling. There in the far corner, she could see a speaker box and a tiny camera. She nudged Drew and pointed.

"I see it." To the camera, Drew mocked, "Too scared to face me yourself?"

"Now, now, Inspector Kelley, don't be a spoilsport." Corben's voice came at them from the speaker. "All in due time."

Keeping her gun at the ready, she faced the camera. "What do you want, Corben? Why have you trapped us here?"

"You trapped yourselves," he countered. "You trespassed."

Sami shook her head. "No, that's not true."

The speaker emitted more laughter, which grated on Sami's nerves. Drew leaned over to whisper in her ear, "Keep him distracted while I work on getting that door open." He tilted his head to indicate the door in the wall.

She nodded and focused back on the camera. "You knew I'd come here."

"I did indeed, Agent Bennett. Or should I call you Sami?"

Gritting her teeth, she ground out, "Sami is reserved for friends and family. You are neither."

She glanced at Drew. He worked on the hinges in the door using her knife, which she'd set on the ground after untying him and Dr. Cantwell.

"True, so true. What is the inspector doing?"

In her peripheral vision, she noticed he had one hinge off. She needed to keep Corben distracted. She moved away from Drew, hoping to draw Corben's attention. Ignoring her captor's question, she asked, "Why did you kill Lonnie? She was your family. She loved you."

"That was unfortunate," Corben said. "After you talked to her, she called me asking me about the murders. She grew too suspicious. Her death is on you." Corben's voice grew hard and menacing.

Sami shook her head. "No way. You can't shift your guilt so easily. I won't accept that. Corben, you need help. Let us help you."

"Like Dr. Cantwell helped me?" Corben let out a bark of laughter. "I shouldn't be too harsh on her. She did help me see how to eliminate my nightmares. It took me a long time to find him, but I did it."

"Find who?" she asked, though she was pretty sure she knew the answer.

"Really, Sami, you haven't figured it out yet?"

"James Clark," she said. "Is he your partner?"

Corben snorted. "No. He's the last person on this earth I'd partner with."

Okay, one question answered. "Is he a victim?"

"*He's* no longer an issue for me."

Now she didn't need that DNA test. "Because you killed him."

"You did find the gift I left you on your pillow, right?"

Her stomach muscles tightened. "Yes."

"Match the DNA. He deserved to die."

She chanced a peek at Drew. He almost had the second hinge off. To Corben she said, "Why did you kill those women? You picked random women to act out your twisted fantasies."

"Not fantasies," Corben countered. "Nightmares."

Sami ruminated on his statement for a moment. Then it dawned on her what he wasn't saying. "You were in the room when your mother was killed."

"Ding, ding, ding." Corben cackled. "I knew you'd be a smart opponent."

She let that go for the moment. "You saw James Clark kill your mother. Why didn't you tell the authorities?"

"I was eight years old. One moment I'm eating pizza and watching television. The next my mom is shoving me into the closet, telling me if I come out, I'll get a spanking like I'd never had before. My mother used a rod for discipline."

Drew had the second hinge off but the door was still in place, looking solid and unbreachable. He turned so that his back was to the camera and met her gaze. He flicked his gaze to her gun and gestured with his head and eyes toward the camera. If she interpreted his message correctly, she surmised he wanted her to shoot the camera so Corben couldn't see them escape.

Torn between wanting to hear more of what motivated Corben and wanting to escape the musty, grimy confines of the crawl space, she acknowledged Drew with a small nod. She had so many questions she wanted Corben to answer. Not the least of which was why he'd killed Lisa. She pushed aside her own need to know and lifted the gun.

"What are you doing, Agent Bennett?" Corben asked. "You think killing my camera will get you out of there? Has Inspector Kelley removed all of the hinges and opened the door yet?" Corben laughed. "No, he hasn't, because if he had, then there would be a big boom. I haven't heard a boom yet."

Drew jerked his hands away from the door and met her eyes with grim disappointment. Corben had booby-trapped the door.

Gritting her teeth, she swung her gaze back to the camera. Fear thudded in her veins. "So you're going to blow yourself up along with us?"

"If I have to."

Their plan to escape just flittered away.

THIRTEEN

Drew's clenched hands ached. He could see despair filling Sami's blue eyes after learning their way out was booby-trapped. His heart ached from not being able to protect her, even though he knew she'd protest the notion.

Ducking low to keep his head from hitting the ceiling and throwing a quick glance at the still-unconscious doctor, he stalked the short distance to the camera and reached up.

"Inspector!" Corben's sharp protest echoed in the tight space. "Don't do that."

Sami nodded and gave him two thumbs-up. Admiration for her mushroomed in his chest. Along with tender affection.

She wasn't like any other woman he'd ever met. Certainly nothing like his ex-wife. Sami was loyal to a fault, honorable and committed. She threw her whole self into everything she did. And he would move mountains, or defuse a bomb, to make sure she left this hole in one piece.

The fire of determination roared bright inside him. With a smile at the camera, he ripped the offending orb out of the wall.

"No!" Corben screamed obscenities at them.

"If you want to finish this twisted game, you'll need to face me like a man." Drew ripped the speaker out of the wall, as well. Now Corben couldn't see, hear or talk to them.

"Drew?" Sami stared at the floorboard overhead, from which she could hear Corben's screams of rage and hear him stomping about. "What if he decides to blow us up?"

"We don't know if he's telling the truth or not," Drew said. "But if there is an explosive device attached to the door, I'd better defuse it and fast."

"You can do that?"

"I've had advanced explosive ordnance disposal training." He moved back to the door and sent up a prayer that it would be enough to thwart whatever Corben had placed outside the door.

Carefully, he inspected the edges of the door and frame. He maneuvered the door to the right until there was a gap on the left side near the bottom where he'd removed the hinge. "Can you hold the door just like this? Don't let it slip or move at all."

Sami grasped the edges. "Thanks. No pressure or anything."

He flashed her a grin, liking her wit and her bravery. He pressed as close to the gap as he could, peering out. He could just make out the shape of a box on the floor in front of the door. A cord attached to the box ran up toward the door, probably wrapped around the door handle.

He sat back on his haunches and took the door back from Sami, easing it back in place.

"Is there a bomb?" she asked, realizing the house had gone eerily silent. What was Corben up to now?

"There's a brown-paper-wrapped package and it's rigged to the door handle. So if the door swings inward, it pulls on the cord, which in turn would trigger a blast, if indeed there is a bomb."

She blew out a noisy breath. "Great. We're trapped in here and no one knows where to find us." She sat down on the ground and crossed her legs as if to meditate.

"Your tech knows where we are, eh?"

She brightened. "Right. And in several days, after I haven't checked in, he'll send the cavalry." She shook her head. "Too bad I didn't stuff my pockets with granola bars."

"We'll be out of here long before we starve." He picked up her knife from the floor where he'd laid it before ripping out the camera. "I'm going to need your help again."

Her eyebrows rose. "What do you plan to do?"

"If I can make a gap big enough to reach through and sever the cord, then we can get out of here in one piece."

She inhaled, squared her shoulders, rose to her feet as best she could and asked, "What do you need me to do?"

"I'm going to lift the door again. This time instead of angling it to the right, we're going to the left. I'm going to see if I can make a gap near the door handle to slip the knife through and hopefully reach the cord before it pulls too tight."

"Oh, that's all. Should be a breeze for a big strong man like you. But what if the cord actually sends an electric charge to the bomb?"

He shook his head. "I'm sure it's attached to a pin that'd be yanked out with the force of the door opening."

"How sure?"

"Pretty sure."

She put a hand on his arm. "Do you mind if we say a quick prayer?"

He covered her hand with his. "That's a brilliant idea."

She hesitated. "I'm not even sure what to say." Her voice quivered slightly as she began. "You know what our predicament is and what we need to do. God, Your word says Your grace is sufficient. I ask for Your grace. I ask that our efforts to escape would be rewarded and Your power would be made known through us. Protect us. Guide us. And deliver us from the enemy's plan. In your precious Son's name, amen."

"Amen," Drew repeated. He lifted Sami's hand and entwined their fingers. "In case this doesn't work—"

"Shh, don't even go there," she interjected. "It has to work."

"Though I appreciate your confidence, there's no guarantee that God will answer our prayer the way we want. He could say no—it's time to bring us home."

Sami's brows pulled together. Her blue eyes bore into him. "No, I refuse to believe God would allow us to get this close to capturing Corben and then let us fail. We have to have faith that good will overcome evil, right here, right now."

Drew nodded and brought their joined hands up, resting her knuckles against his chin. "Okay. We'll go with faith because that's all we have in the end, isn't it?"

"When it comes right down to it, yes, that is all we have. And all we need."

He kissed her knuckle before releasing his hold on her. "Here we go."

Grasping the door, he lifted it slightly. Sami moved in front of him so that his arms bracketed her. She placed her hands next to his and took hold of the door. He slowly released his hold, transferring the weight of the door to her.

He moved to the right edge of the door. "Gently, slowly, swing the bottom of the door to the left."

She did as he instructed. He pressed his face to the emerging gap. He could see the slack in the cord growing taut.

"Stop," he said when the cord was almost completely straight.

Blowing out a calming breath, he slipped his hand holding the knife through the tight opening until the blade of the knife touched the black nylon cord. He needed a bit more slack before making an attempt to sever the cord. "Ease the door back into place until I tell you to stop."

"It will pinch your arm," she protested.

"Don't worry about that."

She did as he'd asked. The edge of the door bit into his wrist but the extra amount of slack was worth the pain. "Stop."

The door stilled. With micro-movements, he sawed the blade through the cord. Beads of sweat broke out on his brow and dripped down his face. He blinked when a salty bead dropped into his eyes. His hand cramped but he didn't stop until two halves of cord dropped away.

He let out a sigh. "Yes."

He withdrew his arm, dropped the knife and grasped the door from Sami. Then he set the piece of wood aside.

"You did it." Sami's jubilant cry spread warmth through his chest.

He turned toward her as she launched herself into his arms and hugged him tight. He held her close, his heart pounding and his blood thrumming.

She pulled back to stare up at him. "See, a little faith."

He laughed and gave in to the urge to kiss her. He fit his mouth to hers. For a moment she stiffened with surprise. Then she melted into him, her mouth softening as she kissed him back.

He thought he heard her give a little moan. His ego puffed up until he realized the moaning came from the doctor lying on the floor.

With aching regret, Drew released Sami. He dropped his forehead to hers. "I think the doc is waking up."

"Looks like." She pressed another kiss on his lips and lingered for a moment before murmuring against his mouth, "My hero."

Stunned, he could only stare at her as his lungs ceased to function. He wanted to be her hero. To be the person she turned to with her problems and her successes. He wanted to be the man she loved.

A blush pinkened her cheeks. She ducked to retrieve her knife and slipped it into the sheath inside her boot, then went to Dr. Cantwell's side.

Oh, man, he was treading in dangerous waters with no life preserver in sight. Good thing he could swim. Because he had a feeling he could find himself gladly drowning in Sami Bennett if he wasn't careful.

"Here, let me help you," Sami said to Dr. Cantwell as the older woman struggled to sit up.

Sami tried to focus on getting the doctor upright and not on the fact that her lips still tingled from Drew's kiss. Her breathing was a bit ragged and her blood pulsed with longing. He'd surprised her when his mouth captured hers, but then she'd given over to the heady and delicious feel of his lips pressed against hers. She hadn't wanted the kiss to end.

She knew he'd kissed her out of relief at not being blown to bits. But she didn't care. She liked his kiss, which was why she'd kissed him again. And would cheerfully do so again and again, if given the chance.

She shook her head. When had she become a masochist? There was no possible future where they ended up together. Her head knew it, but her heart didn't want to accept the knowledge. And she refused to look too closely at exactly what her heart did want.

"What happened?" Dr. Cantwell grasped her temples once she was fully in a sitting position. "Oh, my head is throbbing."

"Sit back against the wall," Sami instructed. She slanted a glance at Drew. He was on his haunches in front of the doorway, squinting at the package on the other side of the threshold. Her heart hammered in her chest with renewed anxiety.

"Be careful," she called to him.

He looked at her with a nod. "Always."

Please, oh, please, don't let that thing go off, Sami silently prayed.

She strained to listen for Corben. Had he left the house? Or was he waiting until they emerged so he could pick them off with Drew's gun? A cold knot of dread and fear lodged in her chest, making her lungs burn as she gasped for breath.

"Agent Bennett?"

Pulling herself together, Sami dragged her gaze away from Drew and focused on Dr. Cantwell, who squinted at her. "Where are we?"

Suspicious of the woman, Sami ground out, "Don't you know?"

"No." The doctor moaned again. "The last thing I remember I was in my office."

Surprise nudged aside her wariness. "So you didn't come here voluntarily?" Was the therapist not involved as they'd suspected?

"Of course not." Dr. Cantwell frowned at her. "Where is here?"

Sami rocked back on her heels. "Michigan. Corben Kraft brought you here."

"Corben." The older woman nodded. "That's right. He knocked on my office's private entrance. When I opened the door, he grabbed my arm and I felt a pin-prick." She inspected her arm. "He injected something into me."

"That's new." Puzzled, Sami tried to make sense of Corben's actions. "He used chloroform on his other victims. I guess killing his doctor isn't a part of his plans. Or at least not in the same way he did the other women."

Horror filled the doctor's green eyes. Sami studied her, wanting to believe she was an innocent victim.

Dr. Cantwell's hand went to her throat. "Other victims? As in more than one?"

Fresh rage nearly choked her. "Twenty-two that we are fairly certain of."

"Oh, no." The doctor tried to stand but fell back and closed her eyes. "I should have told you when you came to my office but I couldn't violate his privacy. But now…"

She opened her eyes. There was no mistaking the distress in her green gaze. "Last time Corben came to see me, he claimed to have avenged his mother's death. But he wouldn't say anything more and ended our session early, telling me he wouldn't be seeing me again." She gave a half shrug. "But then, he always says that after each session. He claimed to not want to come see me, but he always showed up for his sessions."

Drew came over and squatted down beside them. "The door leads to a windowless utility room and a short flight of stairs to the main floor of the house. I'll take your gun and see if I can flush Corben out so you two can escape."

Sami shook her head, suddenly terrified of losing him. "No way. I'll go."

Drew's hazel eyes hardened. "Don't fight me on this, Sami. This isn't me coddling you. One of us has to be the bait to draw him out."

She swallowed, unwilling to let him take on this burden alone. "We go together."

A muscle ticked in his jaw. "Not happening. The only way this works is for me to go."

Rioting panic turned her blood to ice. "He has your gun," Sami protested. "He could pick you off the second you emerge."

He nodded, making it clear he'd already run that scenario through his mind.

Tears burned behind her eyes. "No. I won't let you sacrifice yourself for me." She couldn't bear the thought of him hurt or dead.

"Not just you," he said gently.

"Okay, us," Sami amended. "There has to be another way."

"I'll go," Dr. Cantwell interjected, coming to her feet. Though she was shorter than Sami, she still had to duck to keep from hitting her head on the wooden floorboards above them.

"No," Sami and Drew said in unison.

"Let me go first," Dr. Cantwell continued, ignoring their protest. "I can distract him while you two find a way to capture him."

Drew shook his head. "That is definitely not happening. You're a civilian. It's our job to protect you."

"How about we do this?" Sami said, her jumbled thoughts forming a plan. "We all go out together. Dr. Cantwell calls out to Corben. Hopefully, he'll answer, which will give us an idea of his whereabouts. For all we know, he escaped again."

Doubts clouded Drew's expression. She held up a hand. "Hear me out." He inclined his head but he didn't look happy about it. "I haven't heard any footsteps or creaking of the floor above us. If he doesn't answer, then the doctor stays put in the utility room while you and I go for it. We have one gun and one knife. It will have to do."

"Give me your knife," Drew said, holding out his hand.

She took the blade out of the sheath and handed it over.

He grasped the handle and then turned, leading the way out of the crawl space into the dark confines of the utility room. The only sound was their breathing. At the top of the short flight of stairs, another door barred their way.

Though she couldn't see Drew, she heard him try the handle. It was locked.

"Now what?" Dr. Cantwell asked, her voice bouncing off the walls.

"You two stand back," Drew said. "I'm going to bust it open."

Frustrated with him, Sami ground out, "Drew, no."

"I'm not arguing with you," he shot back. "Get back."

Not liking his he-man attitude, she said, "At least take my gun."

"You hang on to it, in case you need it."

Dr. Cantwell tugged at her arm. "Come on, Agent Bennett. Sometimes being a team player means letting someone else lead."

Great, now she was getting it from both sides. Groping for the wall, she and Dr. Cantwell retreated to the far corner.

She heard Drew's grunt as his body slammed into the locked door, then wood splintering as the door gave way. Though Sami couldn't see Drew, she felt his absence keenly deep in her heart. Dr. Cantwell grabbed her hand and squeezed.

Where was Drew?

She held her breath, straining to listen.

There was a scuffling sound.

Then the blast of a gun.

FOURTEEN

Fear exploded inside Sami's chest. The echo of gun-fire pounded through her head. The walls of the utility room closed in on her, fueling her panic. Was Drew hurt? Dead? She needed to help him.

"Stay here," she told Dr. Cantwell.

The stairs led to the kitchen.

Caution forced Sami to press her back to the wall and then peek out. The fact that she could make out the counter and appliances barely registered. The back door was boarded up.

She hurried toward the living room, feeling her way through the gloom that suddenly was chased away by dim light.

The front door stood wide-open, allowing the moon's glow to stream into the house. She recognized the form lying prone on his back in the middle of the empty living room.

Drew!

Her breath stalled with fear. No!

Keeping her head low, she inched out, searching for Corben. Acutely aware that she was putting herself in jeopardy, she moved to Drew's side. Her heart wept.

Guilt chomped through her like a hungry tiger. Not again. Only this was so much worse than when Ian was injured.

Back then she'd felt only anger and guilt, not the despair threatening to rob her of her senses.

"Please, don't be dead," she whispered.

"Not dead," Drew said, though his voice sounded strained.

Tears of happiness filled her eyes. She dropped her chin to her chest. She realized with stark clarity that her feelings for this man went way beyond professional and slid right on into dangerous territory. But now was not the time or place to explore exactly what that territory entailed.

Drew clutched her arm. "He was here."

"Yeah, I kinda figured that." She pulled herself together. "Where are you hurt?"

"Shoulder."

She breathed easier. He probably wouldn't die from a shoulder wound if she stopped his bleeding. "I'm going to take the bandage from your back and put it on your wound."

"No time." Drew pushed at her. "Go after him."

"But you could bleed out!"

"I won't. He's getting away. Now go."

Dr. Cantwell crawled to her side. "I'll take care of him."

Grateful, Sami nodded. Gathering her courage, she pressed her lips to Drew's. "I'll be back."

"I'll hold you to that promise."

With grim determination, she rose and headed out the front door, leading with her gun. On the porch she stopped. She didn't see Corben. She strained to listen for any telltale sign that he was close by. To her left she heard an engine turn over.

She ran around the side of the house toward a detached garage she hadn't noticed when they'd arrived. A black Mercedes-Benz shot out, breaking through the wooden garage door.

She stopped in the car's path, stood her ground, aimed and fired several rounds into the car, shattering the front windshield. The car careened out of control, swerving into a tree.

Sami cautiously approached the vehicle. "Put your hands up!"

Corben didn't comply. Sami got closer, half hoping, half fearing he was dead. There were still so many unanswered questions.

She opened the driver's door. He was hunched over the steering wheel. "Corben, put your hands up."

In a swift move, he straightened, bringing Drew's gun up and aiming toward his temple.

"No," Sami screamed, and rushed forward to prevent him from ending his own life.

He quickly turned the gun toward her and laughed. "Really, Agent Bennett, you thought I'd kill myself?"

Sami skidded to a halt. In the moonlight, she couldn't make out his features.

They were at an impasse. Each aiming a gun at the other.

"Lay the gun down, Corben," she demanded. "Come out of the car slowly."

"You back up," he shouted.

She took three steps back. A strange calmness descended on her, making her hands steady and her voice hard. "Now what, Corben? We shoot each other? Like you shot Drew?"

He slipped out of the car. He was taller than she'd expected. He wore black pants and a black turtleneck underneath a flak vest with two distinct indentations where her bullets had hit their mark.

He had thinning blond hair, nondescript features. Just an average guy. The kind people hardly notice. Casebook serial killer.

He pulled his lips back to reveal straight white teeth. "Nice to finally meet you, Agent Bennett. And you can call me Birdman. I so like that nickname you gave me."

"It isn't an endearment."

He shrugged. "Still, it makes me feel special. You've been on my mind for a while now."

Revulsion curled her lip. "And you've been on mine."

"I know. I've been following you. You and the Mountie." He shook his head. "That was unexpected."

"What was unexpected?"

"You two falling for each other." He snorted. "Now he's dead."

Not acknowledging his statement, Sami tilted her head. He didn't know that he'd only wounded Drew?

"You don't seem too broken up about it," Corben commented. "Curious."

Not willing to let him know he hadn't succeeded in killing Drew, she said, "Tell me something, Corben. Why me?"

"Your hair," he said. "I like your hair."

She made a face, trying to comprehend his answer. "What?"

He stepped toward her.

She gestured with the gun. "Stay where you are."

He stopped, a sly smile on his face. "I was at the symposium on serial killers." He laughed. "I couldn't resist. I wanted to know what you federal agents could teach me. And there you were, with your shiny blond hair. So pretty. So eager to learn. I knew you'd be a good adversary."

His twisted logic made acid burn through her. Her finger flexed on the trigger. But there were still questions she wanted answers to. "What do you mean, you were there?"

"I'm everywhere, Agent Bennett. Haven't you realized that yet? I'm a chameleon. An apparition. Always changing, always evolving. It's easy enough to forge credentials and dress the part of a sloppy detective from some backwater town."

"You're a monster," she shot back. "Why Lisa? Why did you kill my best friend?"

"I had to bring you on board somehow," he said. "She was a fighter."

Sami ground her teeth with fury. She was so tempted to end this here and now, to extract her own form of justice. For Lisa. For all the women Corben had killed.

A movement to the right, behind Corben, drew her attention. Drew. Her heart leaped. He wouldn't approve of her taking matters into her own hands. Seeing him gave her strength to stay focused, calm.

He moved in a crouch to the other side of the vehicle.

She needed to draw Corben farther out, away from the car, so Drew could get in position behind him. She stepped backward. There was a piece of the puzzle she wasn't seeing. "How did you move your victims from place to place without being caught?"

He smirked and matched her step. "Have you ever

flown on a private jet, Agent Bennett? There is no pesky TSA and Canpass is such a lovely thing. Easy to join, easy to qualify and even easier to stash anything I want in the cargo hold of the plane."

She shuddered at the thought. "I can't believe you weren't caught before now."

"Tsk, tsk, Agent Bennett." He shook his head. "It's all about patience. And years and years of painstakingly building trust."

Continuing to move away from him, she asked, "Why did you bring Dr. Cantwell here?"

He frowned and stepped toward her. "I knew she would tell you about me."

"You injected her with something." Sami took another step back.

He followed. "Propofol. I stole some when I visited my aunt at the hospital."

"Lonnie would be so disappointed," Sami said, infusing her voice with as much disdain as she could. "What was on her computer?"

"She kept pictures of me on her computer." He spat on the ground. "I don't like pictures."

Taking another step back, she asked, "Who paid for this house?"

He sneered and matched her step. "He did."

"Do you mean James Clark? Your father?"

"My father." Corben spit on the ground. "He may have spawned me, but he was never my father."

"But he provided a house for you," Sami pointed out.

"Only because he didn't want his real family to know about us."

"Is that what your mother told you?"

"That's what I *heard*."

Dr. Cantwell came out of the house, drawing their attention. Her hair had come undone, the silver streaks winking in the moonlight. "Corben, don't do this."

Keeping the gun in his hand aimed at Sami, Corben looked at the doctor. "You should stay out of this, Dr. Cantwell. I let you live. You should be happy with me."

"Haven't you killed enough people?" She walked toward him, her hands out, palms up in supplication. "I'm sorry I failed you."

Corben's face twisted with confusion. "You didn't fail me. You released me from the nightmares." He cocked his head to the side. "Don't you remember? You took me back to that night and helped me see everything so clearly. That's how I found him. It took me two years, but I did it."

"The regression therapy wasn't intended to make you a killer."

His laughter grated on Sami's nerves. Unfortunately, the therapy that was meant to help had been the catalyst to his murder spree. She continued walking backward.

His gazed whipped to her. "Where are you going, Agent Bennett?"

Still moving backward, Sami asked, "What happened the night your mother was murdered?"

"I'm not telling you." Corben stalked toward her.

Dr. Cantwell moved so that she stood between them. "I'll tell her."

Sami took a step to the side in time to see Corben's expression go from gloating to bewilderment.

"You don't know either," he said.

"But I do," Dr. Cantwell said. "Your mother made you stay in the closet. That's what you told me. She locked you in the closet often, didn't she?"

Sami wanted to feel sympathy for him, but all she felt was pity and anger. Becca Kraft had damaged not only her son but so many other lives.

Corben grabbed his head, the gun now aimed at the sky. "Yes. She made me hide in the closet. She said my daddy was coming and he didn't want to see me."

"But you didn't stay in the closet, did you?" Dr. Cantwell said, her voice gentle and coaxing. "You snuck out and saw a man hurting your mother."

Drew rounded the car and crouched by the front bumper.

"Yes." Corben went to his knees. "He had a knife."

"You never saw his face, though, did you, Corben?" Dr. Cantwell stepped closer to him. Sami matched her steps until the doctor was within arm's reach.

"No, I didn't see his face. Just the bird on his jacket." Corben lurched to his feet. "That ugly bird staring at me. Every night. That bird would attack me. Over and over. Just as he had my mother. There was so much blood."

Sami met Drew's gaze. He nodded, the signal he was going to launch an assault. She sent up a prayer that he'd succeed without any more harm to himself. Keeping her weapon aimed at Corben, she grabbed the back of Dr. Cantwell's shirt and dragged her to the ground.

At the same time, Drew launched himself at Corben, taking him down.

They wrestled in the dirt. Sami's breath caught and held in her throat. She couldn't let Drew do this alone with a wounded shoulder. Jamming her gun into her holster, she piled on the fray, struggling to pin Corben's gun arm down. But he was stronger than she'd anticipated. He wrenched his arm free. She grappled to re-claim her hold, determined to make him yield.

Sirens split the air as several cars came screeching to a halt in the driveway.

The loud blast of the gun going off reverberated inside Sami's head.

Drew and Corben stilled beneath her. There was blood everywhere. Sami pushed back on her heels, scrambling to draw her gun even as her heart froze in her chest. Who's blood was it that ran into the dirt? Was Drew hit? Corben?

Time seemed to slow. A shudder of fear and denial worked its way over her. Neither man moved.

"Drew!"

Please, God, she silently begged. *I can't lose him.*

Drew had worked his way past the barriers of her heart and made her care, made her long for a life beyond the badge. Somewhere along the way she'd lost control of her emotions and fallen in love with him.

The thought knocked the breath from her lungs, and she willed Drew to get up, to be okay.

Finally, Drew pushed Corben's still body aside and stumbled to his feet. He kicked the gun away.

A rush of relief flooded Sami. She tucked her weapon into her holster and flung herself at Drew. He caught her with his good arm. He felt solid and warm and so good. She squeezed her eyes shut, savoring the moment. He swayed on his feet. Concern arched through her. She pulled back to look at him. His face was ashen, his eyes slightly glazed. He'd lost a lot of blood despite Dr. Cantwell applying a bandage to his gunshot wound.

Suddenly Detroit police officers surrounded them. A second wave of relief made her limbs turn to jelly.

"I called the cavalry. I found your cell phone on the living room floor." Drew kissed her quickly and murmured, "We'll finish this later."

It was a promise she would make sure he kept. Paramedics led Drew away to an ambulance while Sami gathered the frayed edges of her composure and reluctantly turned her focus back to the job of dealing with the officers and Corben Kraft.

"Good work, Agent Bennett." Special Agent in Charge Granger beamed at her with approval. The moment the news came of Corben's arrest, Granger had boarded a plane and flown to Detroit. Sami and her superior stood in the conference room of the Detroit FBI field office.

The Federal Bureau had taken over custody of Corben Kraft. Right now he was detained in a secure room until the transport unit was ready move to him to the maximum-security federal prison in Florence, Colorado, to await his trial. Dr. Cantwell had formally diagnosed Corben with antisocial behavior disorder and stated for the record he was both a psychopath and a sociopath, since he exhibited behaviors inherent to both disorders.

Whatever label his mental illness took on wouldn't save him from the punishment he was due. For that, Sami was grateful.

Sami rubbed at a kink in her neck. "It wasn't all me, sir. We wouldn't have captured Kraft if not for Dre… uh, Inspector Kelley."

With Sami and Drew's statements and that of Dr. Cantwell, Corben Kraft was going to prison for the rest of his life. Though his incarceration wouldn't bring back those who'd lost their lives at his hand, there was peace in knowing Corben wasn't free to kill again.

Granger nodded. "Too true. I've spoken to his superintendent, praising the inspector's efforts. You both deserve commendations for apprehending Kraft."

"Thank you, sir, but that's not necessary for me. I was doing my job." Drew, however, had taken a bullet in the shoulder and for that he deserved a medal of valor, a parade…a kiss.

It had been several hours since she'd seen Drew loaded aboard the ambulance and whisked away. The paramedics had been optimistic that the wound wasn't fatal, but she needed to know for herself that he was okay. She glanced at her watch. The last time she called the hospital, she'd been told he was in surgery.

"Sir, I would like to request permission to go to the hospital and check on Inspector Kelley. He should be out of surgery by now."

"Of course," Granger said. "I'm sure Inspector Kelley would be happy to learn that Corben is safely behind bars."

"Yes, sir."

She turned to leave.

"Samantha," Granger called, halting her steps.

She pivoted. "Sir?"

"I thought you'd be interested to know that the Legat in Vancouver has announced his retirement."

"Okay, thank you." Though she wasn't sure why he'd think she'd be interested. It wasn't as if she had the qualifications to apply for the position.

She hurried from the building and hailed a taxi. Once settled in the back passenger seat, she mulled over Granger's comment. With the legal attaché retiring, there would be an opening in the FBI's Vancouver sub office. It was an interesting thought, and maybe in a few years, say in ten or so, she'd be qualified for such a post. But it would be highly unlikely that the new Legat would be ready to vacate the position so she could step into it.

She pushed the notion out of her head as the cab stopped at the front entrance of the Detroit Medical Center. She paid the driver, then walked through the sliding glass doors.

Immediately, she was assaulted with the sounds, the smells of a hospital. Her steps faltered as a terrifying awareness slammed into her. Once again she was visiting someone she cared about, wounded in the line of duty. Who was she kidding? What she felt for Drew went deeper. She loved him.

Anxiety twisted in her chest, making her jittery. The knowledge that she'd fallen in love with Drew simmered in her mind as she forced her feet to move. At the administration desk she was directed to Drew's room on the fourth floor. She found the stairs and hurried up them as if being chased. In a way she was. She had no idea what to do about her feelings for Drew.

With each step the hurdles that stood between them battered at her brain. She lived in Oregon. He lived in Vancouver, BC. She worked for the FBI. He was a Royal Canadian Mountie. Their jurisdictions were far apart, too far for any sort of relationship to last. And she wouldn't ask him to give up his life, his career. Nor could she give up hers, because if either one of them made such a drastic move, she was sure resentment would follow and ruin whatever chance they would have of happiness.

But knowing all the obstacles didn't keep her heart from wanting to be with him. If only she could tell him that she…what? That she'd let him into her heart? That she loved him with an unbridled love that she'd never experienced before, but she couldn't foresee a future with him?

No, she wouldn't be so cruel as to tell him that she loved him. It was better to part as friends and colleagues. She would leave emotion out despite the ache it caused her.

At the nurses' station on the fourth floor, she asked about Drew's prognosis. Because she wasn't family, she had to flash her badge in order for the nurse to relay any information. The nurse told her that Drew had come through the surgery and was expected to make a full recovery. A giant weight lifted off her chest as she made her way to his room.

She halted in the doorway. Drew lay still in the bed with a light blue blanket covering his legs and leaving his chest bare, except for the large white bandage wrapped around his shoulder. A stark reminder of how close he'd come to dying. Twice.

Her breath stalled in her chest and expanded until she thought her ribs might burst apart.

His dark lashes splayed against his cheeks. His dark hair was mussed and a shadow deepened the contours of his unshaven jaw. Monitors beeped, showing his heart rate, his pulse. A bag hung from a hook on a pole and dripped into the IV attached to the back of his hand.

He looked so vulnerable, defenseless, lying there exposed. Her heart crimped painfully inside her chest. She wanted to go to him, to smooth away the lock of hair that had fallen over his forehead. She wanted to take his hand in hers and hang on for dear life.

But she couldn't. It wouldn't be fair to him. Or to herself. A clean break was better. She could communicate her gratitude via email or text. Hating herself for her cowardice, she turned away, intending to slip quietly out of his life, though she knew he'd never be far from her mind.

"Don't leave me."

Drew's slurred words jerked her gaze back to him and seared clean through her. His eyes were open, though his pupils were large and unfocused. He was on pain medication and groggy from his surgery. He couldn't know the impact those three words had on her.

He gave her a lopsided grin that made her female senses hum. Swallowing her trepidation, she moved to his side with an answering smile that she hoped didn't waver despite the tears of regret for what would never be gathering inside of her.

"Hey there," she said. "I didn't mean to disturb you. You need your rest."

"You could never be a bother, but you definitely disturb me."

"What?" Her voice came out in a high-pitched croak. What did that mean?

His grin deepened. "You're so pretty, especially when you're flustered."

She arched an eyebrow. "Oh, really?"

He wagged his eyebrows. "Yes, really."

Though the smart thing would be to back away from his charming magnetism, she stayed rooted to the floor. "You should be resting, not poking fun at me."

"I will rest now that you're here." His fingers groped for her hand.

Unwilling to deny him, she threaded her fingers through his. A fat tear escaped and rolled down her cheek. Stupid emotions. She was supposed to be strong, not weepy. But for some reason she couldn't muster up enough strength to stop the flow of tears.

Drew's brow creased. "Why are you crying? We got him, didn't we?"

Despite her inner turmoil, she nodded and forced some semblance of self-control. "We did." She told him what was happening with Corben and where he would be going.

"Then why are you sad?"

There he went again. Perceptive, as ever. She struggled to find the right words. "I was so scared when I heard that last gunshot. I—" Her throat closed, trapping her in thoughts of all the horror they'd gone through.

Finding body after body, chasing down a psychotic killer, trapped with an explosive device and then confronted with a madman wielding a gun was more than most people encountered in a lifetime, let alone the course of several days.

Recalling the sight of Drew wrestling with Corben for possession of the weapon made sweat break out on her brow. She'd never been so terrified of losing anyone.

"Hey, it's okay. I'm fine." He squeezed her hand. "I know how hard it must be for you to come here. I know you don't like hospitals."

She wiped at her tears with her free hand. "No, I don't. Ever since Ian's injury." She bit her lip, reliving that moment when she'd entered his room and seen the damage done to his leg. A career-ending injury that could have been avoided if she hadn't allowed their relationship to turn personal.

A little voice inside of her whispered that she'd let her relationship with Drew turn personal and they'd both survived.

But things could have easily turned out differently, she argued.

Drew gave her a look that could have curdled milk. "Excuse me, but I'm not Ian. And this—" he gestured with his chin toward his wounded shoulder "—isn't the end of my life nor my career."

"Thank God for that," she said, meaning it. She'd prayed for His protection over them and He'd kept them alive. But she was afraid to count on God again. What if next time—

"Exactly." Drew's intense gaze made her feel slightly off balance. "Faith will see us through."

She wanted to believe him with every fiber of her being. But she was a realist. They didn't have a future together. And prolonging the inevitable was torture. "I should go and let you sleep."

His eyelids fluttered. "I'd rather you stayed."

"There's still a great deal of red tape to sort through, so I don't know if I'll be able to get back here. Both of our countries want to prosecute Corben."

Drew's eyes closed all the way. "Your collar."

She was glad he couldn't see the tears again gathering in her eyes. He was so selfless, so caring. A man of honor and integrity. Her heart ached with loss. Though she couldn't resist leaning in to place a kiss on his lips, imprinting this moment in her mind.

"Hmm," he murmured, drowsily. "Nice."

"Thank you," she whispered. "For everything."

His even breathing told her he'd fallen asleep. She backed away until she hit the door. "Goodbye," she breathed out, feeling as if a part of her was dying.

She turned and fled.

Sami's cell phone rang, jerking her to awareness. She was at the airport, waiting to board a plane heading back to Portland, Oregon. Corben had been transported via a heavily armed escort to Colorado. Granger had gone along to finish the processing at the prison. Sami was free to go home.

Only she didn't feel right leaving with Drew still in the hospital.

But she'd made her choice. She couldn't keep hanging on to him. She couldn't pretend that there was a future where they ended up together.

She shifted in the hard plastic seat of the waiting area and dug her phone out of her pants pocket. "Agent Bennett here."

"Agent Bennett, uh, Sami, this is Sergeant Kelley, Drew's father."

She sat up. "Hello, sir." Her mind reeled. Had something happened to Drew? Had he had a relapse? Her pulse pounded in her ears. "Is there a problem?"

"No, I don't think so." Yet he sounded concerned. "I wanted to talk to Drew's doctor about his prognosis and when he would be discharged, but the hospital wouldn't release information to me over the phone."

"Did you try calling Drew's room?" She stood and picked up her small bag. Her feet were moving away from the gate before she'd even realized she'd made the decision she wasn't leaving Detroit. Not without Drew.

"I did, but he's been groggy and unhelpful. All he wants to talk about is you."

Surprise washed over her. She wasn't sure how to respond. "Uh, well, sir, I'm on my way to the hospital. I'll call you from there once I know more."

"I would appreciate it," he said. "And please call me Patrick."

"Patrick it is, then," she said as she left the airport terminal and got in line for a taxi. She told the attendant where she wanted to go. He waved the next taxi forward and she climbed inside.

"Sami, my son has been hurt in the past," the older man's voice dropped an octave. "We both have."

A vice-like clamp squeezed over her heart. "Drew told me about his ex-wife. And a little about his mother."

"She walked out on us when he was just a boy," Patrick said. "It was hard on him. On us."

Fresh tears pricked her eyes and she hurt for Drew and Patrick. "I can only imagine."

"Yes, well, it left scars." He cleared his throat. "Drew is very taken with you. He doesn't trust easily. And I sense you're different."

His words eased the pressure around her heart and tenderness flooded her. "I care for him, too."

"But do you love him?"

The pointed question rammed into her like a fist. She swallowed back the fear that reared up, making her want to cut off this conversation.

Drew had told her that faith would see them through. Could faith, could God, make a way for them to have a future, too? Was she brave enough to take a chance?

"Sami?"

She squared her shoulders and faced the truth. She

never backed down from a challenge or a fight. And Drew was worth fighting for. "Yes. Yes, I do."

"Good."

And it was good. She had no idea how the future would work out. Maybe that was for the best. She'd have no preconceived ideas or expectations. All that mattered now was telling Drew how she felt. And pray he felt the same.

Three days later, after surgery to remove the bullet lodged in his shoulder and another round of stitches in his back, Drew was discharged from the Detroit hospital. He'd called his dad, who'd said he'd fly in to get him. He'd been given scrubs to wear home. After helping him into the shirt, the nurse, thankfully, left him to finish dressing himself.

He'd already given his statement to the local police and the federal agents from his hospital bed. Sami had come to see him right after the surgery. He'd been too medicated for any real conversation that he could recall, so he had no idea when he'd see her again. He did remember she looked tired, and maybe sad, but his memory was a bit fuzzy. He did know that. Corben was behind bars. They'd put an end to his killing spree.

Sami had explained she'd be bogged down in red tape for a while and didn't know when she'd see him again. He vaguely remembered her using the word *if*. On one hand, he'd understood; this was her case to close. And on the other hand, he was afraid that was her way of saying goodbye.

He didn't want goodbye. He wanted forever.

He missed her something fierce. When the time was right, he was going to see her again, kiss her again. Take her on a date, spend time with her without bad guys or the threat of an explosion to distract them. And he wasn't going to take no for an answer.

A nurse knocked on the door to his room. "Inspector Kelley, your ride is here."

The nurse insisted he sit in the wheelchair. Hospital policy, she said. At the entrance, it wasn't his dad who stood waiting for him. He blinked, sure the sunlight was making him see what he wanted to see. His heart danced in his chest.

Sami leaned against their rented sedan. She was beautiful with her blond hair cascading over her shoulders. She had on green cargo pants, black boots and a ruffled top in a light pink color. The conflicting styles made him grin. So Sami.

A rush of pleasure and something else, something he could no longer deny, flooded him. Her bright smile made his blood race and his breath catch. Not taking his gaze off her, he stood, thanked the nurse, then headed toward the woman he'd fallen in love with.

Somewhere between catching her at his stakeout and seeing her so bravely face down Corben, Drew had acknowledged something his heart had accepted already.

He loved Sami.

He still couldn't believe she was alive and in one piece. When he'd managed to get himself up off the floor after he'd been shot and get out of the house, he'd seen Sami and Corben in a standoff. His heart had fallen and his first inclination had been to charge out there to protect her.

Instead he'd waited for the opportunity to disarm Corben. Shooting him hadn't been Drew's intention. At first Drew hadn't realized Corben had on body armor, but he had and it had saved his life.

"Hi," he said, halting in front of her.

"I'm sorry I wasn't able to come see you sooner," she said.

"You're here now," he replied, wondering how to get past this awkwardness. "Where's my dad?"

Her blue eyes twinkled. "Oh, we have an understanding."

He arched an eyebrow. "Do tell."

"He'll meet us when we land in Vancouver." She opened the passenger door for him. "Sir, your chariot awaits."

She was going to Vancouver with him? Fabulous. He stayed rooted to the spot, drinking her in. Love expanded in his chest until he thought he might burst out in a love song like some Broadway musical. The thought amused him even as he struggled to find the words to tell her how he felt.

"Is something wrong?" Uncertainty crossed her face and dampened the bright light in her eyes.

With his good arm, he reached for her, pulling her close. He'd rather show her how he felt. He kissed her, putting all the love in his heart into the kiss. After several long heartbeats, she pulled back and stared up at him with joy beaming on her pretty face.

"With you by my side, there could never be anything wrong," he said softly.

She placed her hand over his heart. "Do you mean that?"

He covered her hand with his. "I do. With my whole heart."

She took a sharp inhale. "I feel the same way."

Delighted to hear those words, he nuzzled her neck and teased, "Oh, what way is that?"

With both of her hands, she cupped his face and made him lift his head until their gazes locked. "We need to talk."

He stilled, his happiness deflating to a pancake. "Uh-oh. That doesn't sound good."

The intensity of her expression made his mouth go dry.

"I don't want our partnership to end."

A fresh jolt of elation spread through him like the sunshine on his back. "That sounds promising."

"There are details we'll need to figure out. Logistics."

He nodded. "Yes, that's true, considering we live in different countries. But honestly, I was hoping for something more than a working relationship."

Her gaze narrowed but a smile played at the corners of her mouth. "Oh, really? Like what?"

"Love and marriage, kids." He grinned. "What better way to bring our two countries together?"

She laughed, a warm sound that he couldn't wait to spend the rest of his life listening to. "I love you, Inspector Kelley."

"Good thing, Agent Bennett, because I happen to love you, too."

He kissed her with the certainty that whatever obstacles they faced would be resolved with love and faith.

EPILOGUE

Two Months Later

"Are you ready to do this?" ICE agent Blake Fallon asked, angling his shoulder against the heavy wooden door. "Time's ticking away."

"Yeah, yeah." Drew held up a hand. "Just a sec."

"He's as impatient as ever," Sami muttered, but there was a bit of affection in her tone.

"He gets the job done," he reminded her. "And he always has our backs."

"True."

Drew smiled at the woman he loved. "Are you ready?"

"Does nervous count?"

He smoothed back her hair and tucked it behind her ear. He couldn't help lingering to cup her cheek. "We've done the hard part."

"True." She checked to be sure she had everything she needed. She moved gracefully; he could hardly believe she was nervous at all. "I'm ready. You?"

"More than." He glanced at the closed door. "You know it will be chaos inside."

"We'll probably get separated," she said laying her hand on his arm.

His fingers curled over hers. "Not for long. We get in, we get out. There's a plane waiting for us at the airport."

"I don't think it's going to be that easy." She adjusted the collar of his jacket with a tender smile. "You know I love a man in uniform."

"Any man?"

"No, just you." She went on tiptoe and kissed him deeply.

"You keep that up, we'll never make it inside," he murmured against her lips. He could lose himself in her kiss and planned to when this was over. But for now, they had their parts to play.

Pink tinged her cheeks. "Okay. Let's do it."

They approached the doors. Tension knotted the muscles in Drew's shoulders. He nodded to Blake.

With a flourish that surprised Drew, the normally sardonic Blake pushed opened the door and his voice boomed out, "The bride and groom."

A cheer rose, rattling the rafters of the large reception hall.

Sami, stunning in her white dress made of lace and silk, pressed close as they made their way inside with the wedding party filing in behind them. So many friends and relatives pressed in to congratulate them. The joy of their union had everyone smiling. Drew could hardly believe that fifteen minutes ago he and Sami had said their marriage vows before God and their friends and family.

They were now husband and wife.

Carefully, maneuvering through the guests, Drew led Sami to the buffet table. He wanted to get the festivities moving along so they could start their honeymoon. The wedding planner had said they needed to be first through the catered buffet line before the guests could eat. Drew wasn't sure about anyone else, but he was famished. Getting married was exhausting and wonderful and scary all at the same time. Even though he'd done this once before, this time around he knew without a doubt Sami was forever.

He would never regret saying *I do* to the bravest, sweetest and most challenging woman he'd ever met. He was proud to call her wife and friend.

And now that she'd taken a job with the FBI sub office in Vancouver as assistant to the new legal attaché, they were house hunting. Or rather, as soon as they returned from their Caribbean honeymoon, they would find a place to call their own, beginning their life together as partners in the truest sense.

* * * * *

Dear Reader,

Sometimes stories come fully formed and are easy to write. This was not one of them. This story came in spurts and spits, taking me in directions I hadn't anticipated. The most of which was the villain. Researching serial killers was the stuff of nightmares, which I had plenty of while writing this book. For that reason I knew I needed two very strong characters who would rise to the challenge. And what a challenge it was for Sami and Drew.

They were led on a twisting and turning chase through two countries, facing numerous obstacles blocking the way. They survived explosions, gunshot wounds and times of deep darkness, but eventually their tenacity and perseverance and faith won the day and they emerged victoriously into the light.

I pray that whatever darkness you face, whatever obstacles you encounter, you will find the light in God's love to lead you into victory.

Look for my next Northern Border Patrol book sometime around the holidays in 2015.

Until we meet again, may God bless you abundantly,

REQUEST YOUR FREE BOOKS!

2 FREE RIVETING INSPIRATIONAL NOVELS
PLUS 2 FREE MYSTERY GIFTS

Love Inspired®

SUSPENSE

RIVETING INSPIRATIONAL ROMANCE

YES! Please send me 2 FREE Love Inspired® Suspense novels and my 2 FREE mystery gifts (gifts are worth about $10). After receiving them, if I don't wish to receive any more books, I can return the shipping statement marked "cancel." If I don't cancel, I will receive 4 brand-new novels every month and be billed just $4.99 per book in the U.S. or $5.49 per book in Canada. That's a savings of at least 17% off the cover price. It's quite a bargain! Shipping and handling is just 50¢ per book in the U.S. and 75¢ per book in Canada.* I understand that accepting the 2 free books and gifts places me under no obligation to buy anything. I can always return a shipment and cancel at any time. Even if I never buy another book, the two free books and gifts are mine to keep forever.

123/323 IDN GH5Z

Name _____ (PLEASE PRINT)

Address _____ Apt. #

City _____ State/Prov. _____ Zip/Postal Code

Signature (if under 18, a parent or guardian must sign)

Mail to the **Reader Service:**
IN U.S.A.: P.O. Box 1867, Buffalo, NY 14240-1867
IN CANADA: P.O. Box 609, Fort Erie, Ontario L2A 5X3

**Are you a current subscriber to Love Inspired® Suspense books
and want to receive the larger-print edition?
Call 1-800-873-8635 or visit www.ReaderService.com.**

* Terms and prices subject to change without notice. Prices do not include applicable taxes. Sales tax applicable in N.Y. Canadian residents will be charged applicable taxes. Offer not valid in Quebec. This offer is limited to one order per household. Not valid for current subscribers to Love Inspired Suspense books. All orders subject to credit approval. Credit or debit balances in a customer's account(s) may be offset by any other outstanding balance owed by or to the customer. Please allow 4 to 6 weeks for delivery. Offer available while quantities last.

Your Privacy—The Reader Service is committed to protecting your privacy. Our Privacy Policy is available online at www.ReaderService.com or upon request from the Reader Service.
We make a portion of our mailing list available to reputable third parties that offer products we believe may interest you. If you prefer that we not exchange your name with third parties, or if you wish to clarify or modify your communication preferences, please visit us at www.ReaderService.com/consumerschoice or write to us at Reader Service Preference Service, P.O. Box 9062, Buffalo, NY 14240-9062. Include your complete name and address.

LIS15

SPECIAL EXCERPT FROM

Love Inspired.
SUSPENSE

Can the Capitol K-9 Unit find Erin Eagleton and solve the mystery of her boyfriend's death before it's too late?

Read on for a sneak preview of
PROOF OF INNOCENCE,
the conclusion to the exciting saga
CAPITOL K-9 UNIT.

An urgent heartbeat pounded through Erin Eagleton's temples each time her feet hit the dry, packed earth. She stumbled, grabbed at a leafy sapling and checked behind her again. The tree's slender limbs hit at her face and neck when she let go, leaving red welts across her cheekbones, but she kept running. Soon it would be full dark, and she would have to find a safe place to hide.

Winded and damp with a cold sweat that shivered down her backbone, Erin tried to catch her breath. Did she dare stop and try to find another path?

The sound of approaching footsteps behind her caused Erin to take off to the right and head deeper into the woods. She had to keep running. But she was so tired. Would she ever be free?

Memories of Chase Zachary moved through her head, causing tears to prick at her eyes. Her first love. Her high school sweetheart who now worked as a K-9 officer with an elite Washington, DC, team. A team that was investigating her.

From what she'd read on the internet and in the local papers, Chase had been one of the first officers on the scene that horrible night.

She'd thought about calling him a hundred times over these past few months, but Erin wasn't sure she could trust even Chase. The last time they'd seen each other last winter, on the very evening this nightmare had taken place, he hadn't been very friendly. He probably hated her for breaking his heart when they were so young.

But then just about everybody else along the beltway hated her right now. Erin had been on the run for months. She knew running made her look guilty, but she'd had no other choice since she'd witnessed the murder of her boyfriend, Michael Jeffries, and she'd almost been killed herself. The authorities thought she was the killer and until she could prove otherwise, Erin had to stay hidden.

Don't miss
PROOF OF INNOCENCE
by Lenora Worth,
available August 2015 wherever
Love Inspired® Suspense books and ebooks are sold.

LISEXP0715